ON BRIGHTON STREETS

By Nisse Visser & Cair Going

On behalf of Invisible Voices of Brighton & Hove,

as part of the BRIGHTON FRINGE FESTIVAL 2018.

All proceeds from this book have been pledged to

Cascade Creative Recovery, First Base & Sussex Homeless Support.

Dear Mike,

Hope you enjoy
the read,
Nis Nisse Visser

Enjoy
Reading.
Cair

On Brighton Streets

By Nisse Visser & Cair Going

Published by CBS Green Man Publications, in May 2018,

on behalf of Invisible Voices of Brighton & Hove,

as part of the Invisible Voices programme

for the 2018 BRIGHTON FRINGE FESTIVAL.

Paperback ISBN: 9789082783643

Kindle E-Book ISBN: 9789082783650

(NUR CODE 270)

Authors: Nils Visser & Cair Emma Going

Cover images

Background image Brighton Pavilion by Dominic Alves, CC2.0

Image Amy & Frances by N.Visser

This book is dedicated to the memories of Iain and Nick, both of whom tragically died, homeless, in Brighton & Hove in March 2018.

CONTENTS

PART ONE

PART TWO

PART THREE

PART ONE

1. The Seagull on London Road

The seagull made Amy Wheatley smile. It was taking dainty steps around an overflowing bin on the pavement, pretending to take no interest in the rubbish just above its head. Every now and then, it would stop and crane its neck, looking this way and that, to see if it was being watched, before daring a quick upwards peek. Its little eyes would widen comically when it regarded the buffet above, but then it would be distracted by some noise; the roar of a passing vehicle, the footfall of shoppers passing by, or the screeches of other gulls soaring over the London Road shops. The gull would then quickly look away and circle the bin again, whilst ignoring the potential treasure trove entirely.

An undercover seagull, Amy thought, amused by her own insight.

"And is that your little girl?" A woman's voice sounded behind her, by the Co-Op supermarket entrance. "My, my, hasn't she grown?"

Reluctantly, Amy tore her eyes away from the seagull and turned around. The woman was standing next to Amy's mother, whose hands rested on the handles of the pram which contained Amy's baby brother Jacob.

The woman had hailed them when Mum, Amy and Jacob had come out of the Co-Op. Amy had gathered she and Mum were old friends who hadn't seen each other for ten years or so, after which Amy had been too distracted by the seagull to pay the grown-ups much attention.

Amy smiled politely at the woman, because it would have been rude to do what she wanted to do, namely roll her eyes at the comment. Adults were forever telling her she had grown since they last saw her. It was as if they didn't know what else to say to children.

"I met you a long time ago," the woman said. "I don't suppose you remember?"

Amy shook her head, with another smile which she hoped was polite and apologetic at the same time. She thought it was a foolish question. If this woman hadn't seen Mum for ten years, then Amy would have been Jacob's age, one-and-a-half, when they had met, or even younger.

"All of eleven years old," Mum said. "Time passes by so fast."

"Eleven-point-five," Amy said, sharper than she intended to.

"What's that Sweetie?" Her mother asked.

"I'm eleven-point-five," Amy explained. "Which is nearly twelve."

"How sweet." Mum's friend laughed. "To use decimal points. When I was young we said 'and-a-half'. Is this a digital generation thing?"

"The digital generation!" Mum laughed. "No, this is one of her very own home-grown quirks."

She laughed again, but it wasn't her real laugh, instead it was the one she used to pretend something was funny when she didn't think it was funny at all. Amy didn't like that laugh, it seemed so fake that it left her feeling embarrassed on her mother's behalf. Amy wondered if her own polite smiles were just as obvious.

Mum followed up her make-believe laugh with a brief stern look at Amy. "Eleven or eleven-and-a-half...it hardly matters, Sweetie."

Amy shrugged. It mattered a great deal to her. There was a big difference between eleven and, say, eleven-point-two-five, and definitely eleven-point-five. She was already counting the days when she'd turn eleven-point-seven-five, which was practically twelve.

"Oh dear." Mum's friend sympathised. "She'll be a moody teenager soon."

"She's headstrong as it is." Mum sighed. "I sometimes wish they weren't in such a hurry to grow up."

Amy offered another smile, trying to make it as sincere as she could. This was another one of those observations that adults seemed to like, often accompanied by promises of imminent doom and gloom. If these were to be believed, Amy would turn into some kind of horrible monster before too long, terrorizing her parents for years on end before it was over. Sometimes Amy would wake up in a panic, and rush to the mirror to see if she had sprouted fangs or horns during the night. All she was ever greeted by, however, was the sight of her unruly red hair pointing every which way, and her freckles of course, scattered across her cheeks, nose and forehead. Luckily, Jacob burped loudly, earning himself the full attention of both Mum and her long lost friend.

Sometimes Amy would feel guilty, when she caught herself hating the amount of attention Jacob received. She was sure only a horrible person would think of a baby brother like that. All the more so because Jacob had just done her a favour, taking the attention off Amy, before Mum and her friend started making embarrassing jokes about boyfriends. That, or the usual about how much Amy looked like Mum, which Amy reckoned was mostly because they both had red hair.

She turned her attention back to the seagull, which was still hopping around the bin. Amy sometimes heard people in Brighton complain about the city's many seagulls, describing them as a dangerous nuisance, but she thought this was silly. Amy liked seagulls. As far as she was concerned, the city wouldn't be the same without their outraged screeches and forlorn cries.

She loved to watch them whirl in winged clouds above the streets and parks, or the seafront, making noises that sounded like mocking laughter. The seagulls clearly thought all those busy and self-important humans below were just a funny joke.

She envied their carefree attitude. Wouldn't life be so much better flying freely through the skies? The feathered pirates of the Sussex coast did as they pleased, free of teachers and homework, free of ten-thousand-and-more rules that had to be obeyed at home and school.

Seagulls poop on rules.

Amy giggled at the thought. The bird by the bin must have heard her, for it gave Amy an outraged look, and then spread its wings and took to the cold and grey winter sky.

Glumly, Amy watched it fly away. The bird had been fun to look at. She briefly focused on the conversation between Mum and the long lost friend. They were no longer doting on Jacob. Instead, they were running down a long list of people they both knew, commenting on their welfare, lingering longer over cases of divorce, ill health, and unemployment.

Amy sighed. There was no sign that the unexpected re-union between the old friends would be over any time soon. She decided to practise smiling at the passing traffic. She would probably need to smile her disappointment away in a bit.

Amy had been delighted earlier in the week, when Mum had announced that she was taking a rare Wednesday afternoon off from her work at a solicitor's office, so that they could have some mother-daughter time. Mum was usually so busy these days, either with work or with Jacob that they didn't get to spend much time together anymore.

Even better, Mum had agreed to take Amy to the Open Market. Amy loved to browse in all the odd little shops and stalls there. There was usually music playing and it was always colourful, even on a cold winter day. She had been looking forward to the visit.

When Amy had come home from school, eager to get going, Mum had insisted on getting Jacob from the nursery earlier, so that he could come along. That was alright, Amy had supposed, but after they had boarded the bus to head down Ditchling Road, Mum had also said that they would need to go to the Co-Op first, before they went to the Open Market.

"Just a few essentials. It won't take long," Mum had promised, but the Co-Op had been busy, Jacob had been fussing for attention in his pram which made their progress slow, and it had all seemed to last forever.

Amy took out her mobile phone and glanced at the time. Even if they left this very second, it would be nearing closing time at the Open Market by the time they got there. The magic of the place was gone once the first traders started packing up, making Amy feel more of a nuisance than a welcomed guest.

A little boy in the upper saloon of a passing bus waved. Amy waved back. She saw a twenty-six pull away from the bus stop across the road, headed for Hollingbury. She imagined what would happen if Mum and her friend just kept on talking and talking. It would get dark, the shops would close, London Road deserted after the last night-bus passed. At some point Dad would be worried sick and call the police to report his wife and children missing.

Amy sighed. Dad would be locked up in his study as usual. He worked at home, but she suspected she'd see him more often if he just worked in an office somewhere. He'd be chasing deadlines, unaware of the world around him, and certainly not realising that his daughter was in terrible danger, likely to die of sheer boredom any moment now.

Perhaps he would find the time to come to her funeral. Amy wanted lots of flowers, like at Gran's funeral, and her parents so broken by grief and regret that they would totally ignore Jacob, no matter how loud her baby brother would be howling for attention.

She might just have to make a list of the music she wanted played. She couldn't possibly leave that up to her parents, they'd probably...

...Someone behind Amy sneezed. A loud explosive sneeze that was repeated twice more, just as Amy spun around to see who was behind her.

2. An Unexpected Meeting on London Road

Amy had previously noticed the big pile of bedding heaped up against the wall below the big Co-Op windows, but had seen nothing but filthy duvets, old blankets, and torn sleeping bags. Now Amy stared in surprise as a woman emerged, untangling herself from the heap.

The woman wore a torn wool jumper, faded into an unidentifiable drab colour, and a green army coat. Her red hair hung straggling and lack-lustre. Amy was puzzled by the woman's face. She found it hard enough to determine the exact age of grown-ups, other than recognising a difference between youngish, oldish, old, and old-old. This woman's face was like a kaleidoscope containing every degree of age. There were echoes of a lively energy suggesting she was youngish, but the expression was that of a hard and guarded mask, like that of most people her parents' age. The woman's eyes, now that they were gaining focus, were green, just like Amy's, but filled with infinite sadness. Enough sorrow to fill several lifetimes. They reminded Amy of Gran's eyes.

One of the woman's cheeks was bruised, a large ugly blue-black mark. There was a cut on her forehead, the red scab angry and festering. Her lips were cracked, and there was a sore in one corner of her mouth.

Amy wanted to take a step back towards the safety of Mum, but decided that was something a young child would do, not somebody who was nearly twelve.

The woman blinked groggily at the daylight. "Giz a fag then."

Amy looked around her, but there was nobody else near, unless there were more people hidden underneath the big pile of blankets.

"Come one, just the one." The woman spoke directly at Amy this time. "Giz a fag."

"I d-d-don't have t-t-that." Amy stammered, something she hadn't done for years.

The woman squinted at Amy, finally seeming to register just who was standing close to her nest of dirty bedding. "Nah, I suppose not." She frowned, angrily. "Just my bloody luck."

Amy shrugged, not knowing how else to respond.

"I don't suppose you got any spare change then?"

Amy shook her head.

"Never mind then," the woman grumbled. "Bloody hell, I feel grotty. I must smell like something awful, innit?"

Amy resented the woman's directness a little, but was also fascinated by the plain honesty of her words. She blurted out: "Maybe you should go home and have a shower?"

The woman's eyes narrowed, her mouth formed half-a-snarl. "Are you taking the bloody Mickey? Dissing me?"

Amy was momentarily taken aback by the sudden flash of anger, fighting the urge to take a few steps away from the woman. Then she became angry herself, she hadn't been making fun of the woman at all. "No, I'm not." She told the woman. "I was trying to be nice. It's just...that I always feel better after I've had a shower, that's all."

The woman regarded Amy for a moment, then relaxed a little. "I haven't got a home to go to, do I? Nor a hot shower."

"But...where do you live then?"

"Here." The woman gestured at the nest of blankets and duvets. "Home, Sweet Home."

"That's horrible!" Amy exclaimed.

"Ain't that right," the woman said, her hard mask gaining some animation. "And in the eyes of some that makes me horrible too, don't it? That's why I reckoned you were dissing me just now. You don't know what it's like. I get called all sorts of nasty names, day in, day out."

"Who would do that?"

"Adults, kids like yourself too, especially when they travel in a pack."

"I *do* know what that's like," Amy said softly.

"Oh, for crying out loud," the woman said. "Your place anything like this fine bit of pavement here?"

"I know what it's like," Amy insisted.

Freckle Face, they called me at school. Ginger Freak, or just plain Freckles.

The woman looked sceptical. Amy swallowed. She hadn't told anyone. Not her old friends from primary school, nor her parents. Suddenly she wanted to share all the bottled-up frustration.

"They call me names, at school," Amy said. "Freckle Face, Ginger Freak...other stuff." She indicated her hair, and then pointed at her freckles, before echoing words just spoken by the woman. "Day in, day out."

The woman closed her eyes, her stoic face broken by a brief expression of pain. Amy could now see that the woman really was only youngish-old at most, not ancient, like thirty or older. When the woman opened her eyes again, the hard mask was back, but her eyes seemed a tinge warmer. The woman indicated her own hair. "You do know then. I know what that's like too, Luv, been there, done that. School's rotten, innit?"

Amy nodded eagerly, and then thrilled herself by saying the words out loud. "School is rotten."

The woman nodded curtly. "What's your name, Luv?"

"Amy."

"Mine's Hailey. Never mind the rotters at school, Amy. Red hair is beautiful. 'Kissed by fire', I read that somewhere." The woman indicated a tattered paperback which was peeking out from the fold of a blanket. "The rotters are just jealous. You should be proud of it, just smile at their words, and if that don't work, kick 'em where it hurts. Do that, and you'll be just fine, as long as you don't turn into a rough sleeper like me, innit?"

"What's a rough sleeper?" Amy asked.

"Bloody hell!" The gruffness was back. "Where did they find you?"

"I just asked a question," Amy shot back. "I think I'll go now."

She made to turn around.

"No wait," Hailey said. "You're right, I am not used to...you become...never mind. Rough sleepers are people who don't have a place to live. So we make do with shop doorways, anything that offers a little bit of shelter. There's hundreds of us in Brighton."

"That many?" Amy asked, incredulously. She frowned. Amy had seen people sitting on the street around the city centre before, but on the occasions that she had pointed them out to Mum and Dad they had referred to them as beggars. Their tone had been dismissive.

"It's a funny old world, innit?" Hailey noted.

"But isn't it really cold?" Amy shivered. October hadn't been bad, but November had brought winter's chill to Brighton, usually made worse on a windy day. She couldn't imagine what it would be like having to sleep outside in such weather.

"Cold, wet, and miserable," Hailey confirmed.

Amy was thoroughly confused. It didn't seem right that someone like Hailey was left to her own devices on the cold streets. "Can't anybody help you? Shouldn't there be..."

Hailey shook her head slowly. "Been to the Council, Luv. I'm not from round here, they told me they only help locals, told me to go back home..."

Amy brightened. Home might not always be fun, it could be lonely at times even if other people lived there, but it was dry and warm. She glanced at her mother, who was still absorbed in her conversation. "Maybe you could go back home," she suggested, before blurting out a half-formed plan. "If you haven't got...I've been saving money, it's in my piggy bank. I could come back...after school some time...I don't mind."

That wasn't entirely true. Amy did mind a little. A few months ago, she had visited the City Books shop in Hove. She had found illustrated versions of the *Secrets of the Wyrde Woods* books there. She loved that series, set in a magical wood deep in the Sussex Weald. Amy had also been enchanted by Jen Gifman's bright and vivid illustrations. Hailey's situation, however, was far more pressing. Amy had been daydreaming of those books for months, but suddenly they seemed far less important.

"I don't mind," Amy repeated, firmly this time. "I'll buy you a train ticket, so you can go home."

Hailey smiled for the first time. It was a beautiful smile, but full of sorrow. "You're a sweet girl, Luv. But I can't..."

"But your family...they must be worried..." Amy stalled. She knew that some people didn't have a family. One of her best friends from primary school, Jasmin, was fostered. It hadn't always been easy for Jasmin. Amy had caught her flinching sometimes, when their group of friends talked about their home life. Amy had realised then that some of the things the others took for granted were absent in Jasmin's life.

Now Amy was unsure if mentioning Hailey's family might have been rude, or made Hailey sad by reminding her of something she didn't have.

Hailey's reaction was startling, her eyes lost focus as if she was staring at something far away, something Amy couldn't see. Hailey's upper body slowly rocked to and fro, and she repeated a hoarse whisper. "It's not safe...Not safe...Not safe..."

"Hailey?" Amy stepped forward, worry on her face. She reached out a hand and touched Hailey's shoulder. "Hailey? Are you alright?"

To Amy's relief, Hailey's eyes focussed again. The young woman seemed disorientated for a moment, looking at Amy blankly, but then there was recognition in her eyes. Hailey smiled for a second time, a tentative smile, trembling between hope and uncertainty.

"Sorry, Luv," she said. "Didn't mean to frighten you. Yes. I'm okay."

"GET AWAY FROM MY DAUGHTER!!"

Mum's near hysterical scream behind her shocked Amy, who looked up and around to see her mother charging forward with cold fury on her face. Surprise turned into shock when Mum closed a hand around Amy's upper arm, and then yanked her backwards, away from Hailey.

"I wasn't…I'm not…" Hailey raised her hands, palms outwards, as if to wield off Mum's anger.

"STAY AWAY FROM HER!!"

"Mum!" Amy protested. "Hailey and I were only…"

Jacob began to wail in his pram.

Mum ignored Amy, and even Jacob. "OR I'LL CALL THE POLICE ON YOU!"

Amy was stunned by her mother's anger. Her arm hurt where Mum's clutched it in a tight grip, but she was far more concerned about the venom directed at Hailey, who had done nothing wrong other than chat to Amy. "Mum!"

"Enough!" Mum dragged Amy back to the pram, in which Jacob was still crying his upset.

Mum's friend directed a look of sheer disapproval at Hailey. Three Year 9 girls from Amy's school walked by, giving Amy pointed looks, exchanging glances, and sniggering. Amy felt a blush rise on her cheeks.

As Mum said a hurried goodbye to her friend, Amy threw an apologetic glance back at Hailey.

I'm sorry, she mouthed.

Hailey shrugged, as if it didn't matter to her, but there was raw pain in her eyes.

Mum still hadn't let go of Amy's arm. Pushing the pram with one hand, and pulling Amy along with the other, she made for the road crossing. The three Year 9 girls had stopped walking, and were pointing at Amy's humiliation, laughing at each other's muted comments. Amy looked away from them. They'd probably be calling her *Baby Freckles* at school tomorrow.

"Mum, you're hurting me!"

"You should know better than to talk to strangers!" Mum's voice reminded Amy of unyielding granite. There was no chance to answer, as they joined the press of people at the crossing waiting for the lights to turn green.

Mum let go of Amy's arm. The buzz of chatter around her increased the daze Amy felt...The sudden interruption, the angry shouting, the indignity of being towed like a toddler, the degree of Mum's displeasure...

Amy looked at her mother as Mum bent low to soothe Jacob whose cries were diminishing to sobs. For a moment it was as if she was looking at someone she didn't know, a stranger. Amy had never witnessed that rabid temper before.

A stranger...Of course Amy knew that she should never talk to strangers, that had been drilled into her at an early age, but it had simply not occurred to her to view Hailey as a stranger in that sense.

The lights turned green, they started crossing London Road. Amy looked towards the Co-Op to catch a glimpse of Hailey, but there were too many people walking by for her to see Hailey seated in her bundle of blankets.

"Those people are unpredictable," Mum said halfway across the road. Her tone had lost its anger, sounding weary instead as she made an attempt to explain. "Some of them are half-mad, most of them drunk or on drugs. They can lash out for no reason at all."

Amy shook her head. She hadn't been entirely comfortable in Hailey's presence, it had all been so new and strange, and there had been Hailey's short spell of weirdness, but in an odd way Amy did feel some sort of connection. Also, Hailey hadn't talked to Amy like she an infant that couldn't be expected to understand complicated grown-up stuff. It had been a relief to tell somebody about the name-calling at school and be taken seriously. Someone who knew what it was like, to be laughed at and called names because of the colour of her hair.

Mum didn't notice Amy's silent disagreement, occupied as she was in directing the pram into the flow of people when they reached the pavement. They slowly made their way to the bus stop. Amy looked across the road again, she had a clear view of the pile of blankets now, but Hailey was gone. A second later she spotted her. The young homeless woman was shuffling in the direction of St Peter's, her head bent low in dejection.

"Mum," Amy said. "She was cold. Cold, tired...and hungry I think. Couldn't we have got her a sandwich and a cup of tea?"

"That would just encourage them," Mum answered, quickening her step. "There's a forty-six, if we dash we can catch it."

"Encourage? But, Mum..."

"That's enough," Mum snapped. "You're not to go anywhere near those people again, do you understand?"

Amy nodded unhappily. They boarded the bus. Mum secured the pram. They folded down their seats, not speaking to each other as the bus continued its journey. They remained in that uneasy silence all the way home to Fiveways.

3. Bullies in Hollingbury

The teacher had settled into a monotonous drone and Amy fought off a yawn.

She wondered how she was supposed to show interest in a school subject when the teacher seemed disinterested to begin with. Back at primary school, she had caught on to the fact that the enthusiasm, with which the staff approached most things, was sometimes feigned. Not in the way that Mum's false laugh was fake. Exaggerated a little, would be a better way to describe it. It would be nice if some of Amy's new secondary school teachers would stir themselves into a bit of exaggeration. Or was that a childish thought, not fitting for someone who was nearly twelve?

The teacher ignored the hushed whispers, as well as occasional snorts and giggles. He kept to his narrative like one of those human-robots in the TV shows Amy's father liked to watch on the sci-fi channels. *Androids* they were called.

Amy didn't join in the hushed sounds of distraction, keeping herself as small and quiet as possible.

She had envied her classmates who had made new and immediate best-friends-forever on the first day at the new school. Now she was wary of them. A few months in, and everything seemed to revolve around popularity. Amy struggled to understand this social game. What she had quickly figured out, was that one way to score points was to get a few laughs in by picking on those who suddenly found themselves outsiders. There was *Freckle Face*, of course, but also *Tubby MacTub* for the fat boy who always looked like he was about to burst into tears...*Four-Eyed-Freak* for the girl with glasses which had such thick lenses that they distorted her eyes...*Metal-mouth* for the girl with braces...*Dwarf* for the boy whose growth lingered years behind the rest.

Those other outsiders, Amy saw after a discreet sweep of the classroom, also seemed focused on remaining as invisible as possible, hoping to avoid being noticed by anyone at all, teacher or pupils.

She looked at the open page of her notebook, which was still blank, then at the teacher, but no matter how hard she tried, she could no longer make any sense of what he was saying. Amy picked up her pencil and started doodling on the open page, a better option than looking at the clock for the thousandth time this lesson. That only made time creep by more slowly. Before long she was sketching a seagull that was taking dainty steps around a rubbish bin.

Amy's thoughts turned to Hailey, and her mother's extreme reaction to the young homeless woman. Part of the episode had been spoken about during dinner at home the previous night. Dad had explained some of the things Mum had mentioned during their dash for the bus. He'd said there was plenty of help available, but that many refused to accept that help, preferring to stay on the streets. As long as people gave them money, or bought them some food or a cup of tea, they were able to live that way. After that Amy had understood why Mum had used the word "encourage", but she still found it hard to believe. Hailey had said that she had asked for help, at the Council but that none had been given.

Amy had tried to ask questions, but Mum wasn't having that, displaying some of that fierceness which had so startled Amy on London Road.

"No buts," Mum had snapped. "You're to stay away from those people, and that's the end of it."

Dad had shrugged his agreement.

It had taken ages to fall asleep last night. Amy's mind had kept on replaying scenes from London Road, and she had tossed and turned as her thoughts swirled in circles. She had been worried about Hailey, because she could hear raindrops pattering against her bedroom window, driven by a brisk wind. It would be cold outside, so cold. Amy had struggled to reconcile the logic of her parents' explanations with her strong intuition that Hailey's situation was simply unfair. She had also dwelled on the topic which her parents hadn't raised during dinner: the furious reaction from Mum, the sheer anger she had directed at Hailey, the tightness of her grip on Amy's arm...

The teacher's monotonous soundtrack stopped. Amy tore herself from her thoughts to see that he had turned around and was now scribbling mysterious spidery symbols on the whiteboard. Some classmates around her were copying them into their notebooks, and Amy squinted at the board to try to make sense of them. After an eternity she identified enough letters to see that the top word was probably 'Homework'. She quickly pencilled 'homework' on the bottom half of her notebook page. The top half of the page, she saw with some surprise, was now covered with sketches of seagulls, soaring over rooftops and reaching out for the clouds. Free.

The teacher turned and dropped back into his bored drawl, giving further instructions regarding the homework assignment. It was from these verbal instructions, rather than the illegible scrawls on the whiteboard, that Amy got the gist of the assignment. She hastily pencilled down the vital clues.

Page 34. Exercises 7.4, 7.5 & 7.6. All calculations...

...but she didn't know what calculations, or how, because the bell rang, and her classmates jumped to their feet to stuff their bags with the fury of a tornado, before jostling their way to the door and into the hallway, already crowded by the end-of-school exodus.

Someone banged into Amy's desk, a hand swept her desktop. Her pencil case dropped to the floor.

MY PENCILS!

They had been a birthday gift from Gran. Gran's last present to Amy ever. Several of the precious colouring pencils escaped the case's mad fall, clattering across the floor. Amy quickly got off her seat and knelt down, hoping to save them.

A well-aimed foot descended to crunch two pencil ends, Amy though she could hear the points snap.

"Sorry there, Freckle Face!" A voice sounded above her even as it passed.

Another foot. Another crunch. Another snap. "Oops! My bad, Ginger."

There was laughter. Amy bit on her lip, waiting until all had passed before starting to gather her pencils. She sighed. Being eleven-point-five was much harder work than she had ever anticipated.

"Come on, girl." The teacher said impatiently. "I haven't got all day."

Amy scooped the last of her spilled pencils into their case and put the pencil case in her bag, before gathering her book and notebook. She didn't answer the teacher, she was upset enough and was of the mind that it had been his job to make sure the class didn't exit in a stampede.

The hallways were practically deserted by the time she left the classroom, although they still felt *busy*, the air vibrant from the recent collective burst of energy.

Amy made her way to the main doors slowly, in the hope that most pupils wouldn't stand around in mobs outside for too long. It had been a cold day, the sky grey and full of drizzle, so there was reason for her optimism that most of the kids would drift off home sooner rather than later.

Her thoughts were interrupted by commotion in an adjoining hallway, just behind shut double-doors. Angry voices, loud and harsh. Amy's first instinct was to make herself scarce, but curiosity got the better of her. She crept up to the doors, along the edge of the hallway, where her movement would be less likely to be spotted through the windows which made up most of the top half of the doors. She saw the edges of shapes on the other side, all wearing school uniforms.

"Bleeding-heart Snowflake," a girl's voice snarled.

"Proud of it!" Another girl's voice replied, higher and full of determined defiance.

Amy dared a quick peek, and then a longer look because she saw she wasn't in immediate danger of being seen. Three girls stood with their backs to Amy, facing a fourth, smaller girl.

Although Amy couldn't see their faces, she knew who the three girls were; the same Year 9 pupils who had sniggered and laughed at her on London Road. The fourth girl was a Year 7 pupil, just like Amy, but in a different class and they had never spoken. She was a bit shorter than Amy, had long fair hair, and a lively, elfish face. She was backed up against a rubbish bin, outwardly calm but Amy could see her eyes darting left and right, as if trying to spot an escape route.

One of the Year 9 girls made a lunge for the smaller girl, who deftly stepped aside.

"No, don't touch her!" Another Year 9 girl shouted. "She's gotta have lice and bugs from all of them filthy drunks she hangs around with."

"And dressed in the same rags her dad dresses the street bums in, when she's at home," the third girl sneered. "But she probably thinks that's fashion."

"She smells like a street bum!" The first Year 9 girl laughed. "Snowflake stinks, just like the smelly tramps she loves."

"You stink!" The small girl they called Snowflake responded fiercely. "All of you!"

The first Year 9 girl lunged again, and managed to get hold of the younger girl's bag. A tug-of-war ensued.

"Let it go!" Snowflake yelled.

"What are you going to do about it, Snowflake?" The Year 9 girl pulling at the bag shouted.

"Bring your daddy's addict friends?" One of the other Year 9 girls stepped forwards, reaching for the bag.

"Stab us with their drug needles?" The third girl said, and also made towards the tug-of-war.

Amy stood frozen to the spot. The Year 9 girls scared her. They were much bigger than she was, giants almost, and they liked inflicting verbal and physical pain on the new Year 7 pupils. *Fresh Fish*, Amy had once heard them say, as they pointed at a group of new pupils scurrying by like frightened mice.

Amy's fear, however, was overcome by anger. It was just wrong, three against one, and it could have been Amy herself, cornered and about to lose her bag in an unfair tug-of-war. She recalled the splintered ends of her carefully sharpened colouring pencils, and that thought was enough to make her angry. What right did all these bullies have to make other kids miserable?

She swung open the door she had been hiding behind, and hollered: "TEACHER COMING! TEACHER COMING!"

The Year 9 girls reacted to Amy's words instantly. They released their hold on Snowflake's bag, dashed away a few steps and then walked away from Amy, down the hallway in a casual, nonchalant way, immersed in deep conversation, as if that was what they had been doing all along.

Snowflake clutched her bag, and threw Amy an inquisitive look.

"Quick," Amy hissed, beckoning the girl towards her. "Quick!"

Fortunately, Snowflake understood immediately and rushed to the doorway.

Just then, one of the Year 9 girls turned her head, and looked comically puzzled for a moment, before shouting, "It's just that ginger freak! There is no teacher!"

The other Year 9 girls turned around too.

Snowflake laughed. "Well, DUH!" She turned to Amy, "LEG IT!"

The two swung the doors shut and raced away. Behind them they heard angry shouts, and then the pounding of feet.

"Faster!" Amy yelled. She was exhilarated that her ploy had worked long enough for them to get away. The sense of triumph soaring through her lent her extra speed. The girls burst through the main doors, and rushed past the last stragglers still lingering about outside school. They threw the girls curious looks, but that was the extent of their response.

Amy dared a quick glance behind them as they ran across the school grounds towards the road. To her fright, she saw that the three Year 9 bullies were still in pursuit, running down the steps at the main entrance, fury on their face.

"WE'RE GONNA GET YOU!" One of them shouted.

"Keep...running..." Snowflake urged between breaths.

Amy did just that, but fast as the Year 7 girls were, the larger girls were gaining momentum, threatening to catch up.

Just as they reached the school gates, a battered white van pulled up by the side of the road. A large man leaned over and opened the passenger door, smiling a jovial greeting. Snowflake clutched Amy's arm and pushed her towards the passenger door.

"Perfect timing!" Snowflake shouted at the man. "Enemy in hot pursuit! We need immediate extraction!"

The man threw her a lazy salute. "Yes, Ma'am."

"Go on!" Snowflake encouraged Amy. "Get in."

Amy took one look at the three Year 9 girls, now rapidly gaining on the school gate, and scrambled into the van.

Snowflake climbed in behind her and banged the door shut. She shouted: "GO! GO! GO!"

"Seatbelts," the man said calmly.

"DAD!" Snowflake shook her head in exasperation. "We're in IMMEDIATE and MORTAL danger!"

"You'll be in ten times more immediate and mortal danger, if you don't do up your seatbelt, Missy."

Snowflake secured her seatbelt and Amy followed suit.

"Good on you both." The man smiled. "Extraction in progress. Taking evasive action."

He drove off. Amy looked in the rear-view mirror to see the Year 9 girls come to a halt, shaking their fists at the departing van. Their mouths opened and closed, but the van's engine was noisy and the whole vehicle was rattling, so Amy couldn't hear their shouts. For a moment they didn't seem scary at all, but looked as silly as goldfish, gawping at a wider world without understanding it. Relief flooded through her, and she began to laugh, long and loud, as the van sped away towards an unknown destination.

4. Along Carden Avenue

The other Year 7 girl laughed along with Amy, as the van rumbled and rattled along the road. The girls clutched each other as they shook with peals of laughter. In the end they could laugh no longer, out of breath.

"Perhaps you wouldn't mind letting me in on the joke, Frances?" The big man driving the van asked.

Amy was relieved to hear the girl's name, she had mentally used 'Snowflake' because that was all she had to go on, but it didn't seem right to use any name bestowed by school bullies.

"There were trolls, Dad," Frances said solemnly.

"Three of them," Amy added.

"Big ones," Frances said. "Massive."

"Humongous," Amy confirmed.

"Ugly too," Frances said. "Covered in genital warts."

The girls dissolved in giggles.

"Geni...? Where did you...? Oh, never mind, I prolly don't want to know." Frances's dad shook his head. "I take it you escaped their clutches?"

"They had me cornered, Dad! They were going to roast me over a fire and have me for tea. Then along comes..." Frances's voice tailed off, and she looked at Amy questioningly.

"Amy," Amy quickly said.

"Amy! Amy saved my skin. She tricked the trolls. We escaped from their clutches. We legged it. We made it to the getaway vehicle." Frances ticked off the process of their narrow escape on her fingers.

"The getaway driver showing up in the nick of time, to whisk the Special Operatives away," Frances's dad said. "So if I understand it correctly, I'm the proper hero of this story?"

"Dad!" Frances sounded outraged. "You nearly got us killed because you didn't drive off immediately. We're the proper heroes in this story. You're not a very good getaway driver, to be honest."

"I'll practice," Frances's dad promised. He glanced at Amy. "Pleased to meet you Amy, I'm Tom Greenwood, and, as you may have guessed, I have the good fortune to be Frances's father."

"Pleased to meet you, Mr Greenwood," Amy said.

"Before I make another mistake as rookie getaway driver, is there a place I need to drop you off? A secret rendezvous, or an illicit hideaway? Troll-free, of course."

Amy laughed dutifully, but she felt a sinking feeling at the thought of going home.

"Oh!" Frances came to Amy's rescue. "But Amy is coming along with us…," she stalled, and looked at Amy. "That is…if you want to…"

Amy nodded eagerly.

"I suppose she could," Mr Greenwood said. "Amy, do your parents know?"

"I'll call!" Amy scrambled for her mobile. Mum would ask too many questions, so she phoned Dad instead. As she had hoped, he sounded absent-minded when he answered her call, no doubt his mind was far away in the depths of whatever IT programming task he was working on.

"Can I go to Frances's place, Dad? I'll be home in time for dinner."

"Who is Frances?" Dad asked.

"Frances Greenwood," Amy answered. "A friend. A friend from school."

Amy cast a sideways glance at Frances, when she said 'a friend'. To her relief Frances responded to the words with an elfish grin. Amy tried to send a mental message to her father. *Did you hear what I said, Dad? A friend. I've made a friend at school.*

Amy turned on the loudspeaker, so that her father's next words were heard by everyone.

"Ah, where does she live? How will you get back?"

"Hello there," Mr Greenwood rumbled loudly. "Tom Greenwood here, Frances's father. We live in Patcham, and if it's alright with you, I'll drop Amy off at home tonight at..."

He glanced at Amy.

"Half six," Amy said. They usually ate at half seven, but if she was back at half six, she could make herself useful when Mum came in after she collected Jacob from the nursery.

"At half six," Mr Greenwood told the phone. "I'll keep an eye out on the both of them."

"Splendid, thank you Mr Greenwood," Amy's dad said and disconnected.

"What do you mean, keeping an eye out on us?" Frances complained. "We're not small children."

"A meaningless assurance," Mr Greenwood answered with a wink. "I've got far better things to be doing."

"Good," Frances said.

Amy smiled. She liked Mr Greenwood, he was funny, and she was a little bit envious of the easy-going banter between Frances and her father, but mostly pleased for her new friend. She was also delighted that the day, which had begun in such a dull fashion, had taken such an upbeat turn.

"How was your day?" Frances asked her father. "Did you find Little John?"

"That I did," Mr Greenwood answered with satisfaction in his voice. "He had the shakes, chilled to the bone. Your chilli soup did him wonders. He said to thank you. Kitted him out properly again. Bivvy bag and so much army gear people will mistake him for a soldier."

"I'm pleased he liked my soup!" Frances exclaimed.

Amy was puzzled, not sure what Frances and Mr Greenwood were talking about. She looked out of the window, watching terraced houses pass by. She saw a hunched figure, cocooned in a sleeping bag, sitting at the corner of the small Sainsbury's, and recalled how the Year 9 girls had taunted Frances. *Filthy drunks. Smelly Tramps. Lice and bugs. Drug needles.*

Was this Little John a...

Amy frowned...her parents called them beggars. The Year 9 girls called them drunks and tramps. Hailey had said rough sleeper. Amy liked that better than the other descriptions.

"Is Little John a rough sleeper?" she asked.

"Yes, he's homeless," Frances answered, and then addressed her father again. "And the in-flight meals? Did you get those?"

In-flight meals? Amy found it hard to connect the subject of homelessness with airplane journeys.

Mr Greenwood chuckled. "Twelve-thousand breakfasts, sixteen-thousand pasta meals. Didn't you spot them in the back?"

Amy and Frances craned their necks to peer into the back of the van. Only now did Amy see that it was loaded almost to the ceiling with rectangular white cardboard boxes marked 'fragile' and 'do not freeze'.

"I could use a hand unloading them at The Office," Mr Greenwood added.

"Child labour!" Frances protested.

"Duly noted. How about you, Amy?" Mr Greenwood asked. "Did you ever think you'd be given a chance to carry twelve-thousand breakfasts in your hands one day?"

"No, Mr Greenwood," Amy answered. "I've never thought of that."

"Sounds like a once-in-a-lifetime opportunity then, doesn't it?" Mr Greenwood asked, with a grin on his face.

"Okay, Dad, we'll help," Frances sighed dramatically. "You win. But I want some time to show Amy around The Office."

"Fair enough," Mr Greenwood agreed.

Although that settled the matter, it still left Amy in much wonder as to what kind of work Mr Greenwood did, and what kind of office it was, that required the unloading of tens of thousands of in-flight meals. She pondered this as she looked out of the window. It was mostly still endless rows of terraced houses passing by, but every now and then the view opened up to allow glimpses of the green expanse of the South Downs, rising high over the abrupt end of rooftops. Mr Greenwood seemed to be taking them to the very edge of Brighton.

5. Aladdin's Cave on Crowhurst Road

Mr Greenwood drove the van onto Hollingbury Industrial Estate, which Amy recognised well enough, because she regularly accompanied her parents to the huge ASDA for the big weekly food shop. After they passed the massive supermarket, Mr Greenwood took a turn down one of the smaller side roads which Amy had never really paid attention to. There were various small warehouses, and a number of small lorries or white vans being loaded and unloaded. Sometimes cargo doors had been rolled up, and inside of the spaces behind them Amy could see stacks of boxes or men administering machines.

They hit another side road, which offered access to the parking lot in front of a ramshackle, two-story building. The main part had its sides covered in sheets of corrugated metal, the once white paint peeling. One corner of the upper stories had windows, suggesting offices. The ground floor had several entrances, regular doors as well as cargo doors. There were a few sheds huddled around the building, all constructed of different materials, their colours hues of faded blue, drab grey and dulled dark green. There was no sign with a company name, or anything else that indicated what the building housed.

Mr Greenwood reversed the van, and it huffed and puffed to a shuddering halt, in a row of parked cars and vans, its rear aligned with one of the cargo doors.

"The Office," Frances said proudly, giving Amy an expectant look.

Amy wasn't quite sure what to make of this odd building yet, but Frances was obviously proud of it, so she said: "Wow."

"Work to be done," Mr Greenwood killed the engine and climbed out of the van. The girls did likewise. Mr Greenwood produced a key ring with scores of keys on it, large and small. He walked towards one of the cargo doors, selected a key and unlocked it, before rolling it up to reveal a store room. There were dozens of empty plastic crates stacked up in a rear corner, and some wooden pallets which Mr Greenwood re-arranged to form a low platform.

"We'll stack 'em on the pallets," he said after he walked back to the van. "Breakfasts to the right, pastas to the left." He opened the rear doors of the van. Amy's heart sank when she realised just how many boxes there were. It would take forever to shift them all to the pallets.

Just then one of the regular doors opened, and two men and three women filed out of the building.

"Need a hand, Tom?" One of the men asked. He was short and wiry, with cropped dark hair with streaks of grey in it.

"I figured we'd have a tea break, Big John," Mr Greenwood said. "Enjoy a cuppa while we watch the girls unload."

He gestured at Amy and Frances.

"In your dreams!" Frances snorted. She turned to the group of people. "Thanks a million. Don't mind my dad, he's had sunstroke or something. Twelve million breakfasts to the right, sixteen billion pasta meals to the left, if you please."

Big John whistled as he examined the white boxes piled high in the van. "Quite a haul, Tom."

"Chuffed to bits," Mr Greenwood answered. "Let's get them unloaded."

Many hands make light work. Before too long, the stacks in the back of the van were rapidly diminishing and the stacks on the pallets rising higher. There was much talk between the adults, good-natured banter, as well as references to donations: goods to be collected and deliveries to be made. Kitchen utensils, tools, fresh food, tinned goods, coats, shoes, toys, books, sleeping bags, tents. It was a dizzying amount of information to make sense of.

"What exactly does your dad do?" Amy asked Frances, as they were collecting another pile of boxes from the van.

"Help people," Frances answered.

"Feed them when they are hungry," Mr Greenwood interjected, striding back to the van for another load. "Clothe them when they are cold, try and help them get back on their feet. Sometimes just say 'hello' and listen to what they have to say. They don't get a lot of that."

"Rough sleepers?" Amy asked Frances, as the two made their way into the storage unit, arms laden with in-flight meals.

"Homeless people," Frances answered.

"They're not all rough sleepers." Mr Greenwood said as he caught up with them. "There's thousands in cars, attics, sheds, boats, caravans...Basic shelter, not much more."

They all piled their boxes on the growing stacks on the pallets.

"Bloody cold this time of year too," Mr Greenwood continued. "Certainly nothing you could call a home. Even warmer temporary places like Bed & Breakfasts aren't a home. Just imagine living with your whole family in one single room for months on end."

Amy paled at the mere thought of sharing just the one room with Mum, Dad, and Jacob. They'd all go mad within a week, she was sure. She blurted out: "Do you know a woman called Hailey?"

"Hailey?" Mr Greenwood scratched his head. "Hair as red as yours, hangs around on London Road?"

Amy nodded. "Yes, I think that's the one."

"She's a good girl." Mr Greenwood smiled. "I brought her an army coat last week, with fleece lining. And a bivvy bag to sleep in."

"I saw that coat," Amy said. "Yesterday, outside the Co-Op."

"It's a small world," Mr Greenwood scanned the back of the van, almost clear of in-flight meals now. "I reckon we can handle what's left. You two have done splendid work, thanks. Time for your grand tour of The Office."

"Thanks Dad!" Frances beamed.

"But make it short. There's sorting to be done."

"Aw!" Frances exclaimed. "How much sorting?"

"Mountains of it," her father answered. "So it'll be the shortest grand tour ever."

Muttering about the unfairness of child labour, Frances pulled Amy towards the door the others had emerged from. It opened unto a stairwell, long narrow metal stairs zigzagging up.

"Do all those people work for your dad?" Amy asked as she followed Frances up the stairs, their footfalls causing resonating thunks.

"They're all volunteers." Frances answered. "Big John is still homeless. Kirsty is too, I think. Tamara and Frank were homeless, until Dad helped them out, and now they want to help in turn. Sue has never been homeless, but she said she felt helpless and wanted to do something. She's here almost every day now."

"Oh!" Amy exclaimed. She felt a pang of guilt. Mum and Dad had specifically said she wasn't to spend time with homeless people, yet here she was, unloading a van with some of them. She reckoned it was okay, though, because her parents had painted an image of some kind of drug-crazed fiends. Amy doubted that description applied to the likes of the people helping Mr Greenwood, working hard to unload food so they could feed people. Besides, she reckoned that Mr Greenwood wouldn't let Frances anywhere near something that was dangerous. That was just a feeling. She had only just met them, but it was easy to sense the warmth between father and daughter, and Amy was convinced that Mr Greenwood loved his daughter to bits.

They reached the first floor landing, and Frances opened a door. Amy stepped through, seemingly straight into...

...some kind of Wonderland, it felt to Amy, as she looked around in amazement. They were in a big room, made smaller by boxes and crates stacked up against the walls, and a huge pile of bags, suitcases, carrier bags, and bulging bin bags in the middle of the room. There were a lot of door openings, through which Amy could see corridors or rooms, with more boxes lining walls, as well as overflowing shelving units.

"Come," Frances took Amy's hand and led her around the big central pile and into one of the corridors. Amy followed her new friend into a warren of corridors and rooms. It was like a maze, and often they had to walk single file because heaps of stacked boxes choked the available space.

"What is all this?" Amy asked, when she had overcome her initial astonishment.

"Donations," Frances answered. "People know what Dad does, and they bring him anything they can. It all piles up."

"That's incredible!"

Frances shrugged. "He can't really say no to any of it, because then they might stop bringing stuff."

They passed through a kitchen area, unlike any kitchen Amy had ever seen. There were thousands of tins, mostly soup, but also tinned vegetables. A big gas stove which held huge pans, enough to make food for an army. They exited the kitchen through a narrow corridor between two loads of stacked water bottles.

They emerged in a small hallway, this one with less stored items, because there were no less than six doorways lining the walls, limiting storage space. Peering through one doorway to her left, Amy recognised the big room where they had first come in, with the pyramid of donated goods in the middle. She realised they had been circling it on their progress through the maze.

"Why is that a problem," Amy asked, having puzzled over Frances's answer about donations. She didn't think much more of anything would fit into The Office at all, but from the conversation during unloading, she had gathered that as much went out as came in.

"Not everybody thinks carefully," Frances said. "So a lot of useless stuff comes in, but there's always a few treasures to be found. Dad wouldn't want to miss out on those."

"Useless? How useless?"

Frances laughed. She walked through one of the open doorways. "We call this room 'Aladdin's Cave'."

Amy followed to find herself in a store room that was somewhat ordered. Shelves reached to the ceiling all around, and on them were clear plastic boxes, most of them marked by hastily penned words giving some clue as to their content. The middle of the room, however, was a mess of bin bags and battered carton boxes. Frances rummaged around in one of them, and then lifted out a wig made from multi-coloured metallic strips. She arranged it on her head, and grinned at Amy. "This useless."

Amy nodded, she didn't know all that much after her brief encounter with Hailey, but she doubted that a party wig would do much good against the cold.

Frances bent low to retrieve a long necklace made up of huge fake pearls. "Not sure what they were thinking...or thinking at all."

She hung the necklace around Amy's neck. They both laughed because it reached to Amy's bellybutton, and more fun was had when they found several pairs of high-heeled shoes. The shoes were far too large for them, but they took off their own footwear and slipped their feet into the adult shoes nonetheless. It was hard just to retain balance without falling over when they took their first tentative steps. Diving back into the pile of donations in the middle of the room, they soon found fancy coats, more plastic jewellery, studded handbags, and a black felt trilby hat, which Amy put on to find it was a perfect fit.

When Mr Greenwood entered Aladdin's Cave, he found them prancing about in a mock fashion show.

Mr Greenwood dropped to his knees and bent his head low. "Your Majesties."

Amy couldn't help but grin at the sight of him on his knees, but Frances nodded at him in a regal fashion, and then stuck her chin in the air. "Indeed, I am Princess Snowflake."

"I am Lady Freckles," Amy chimed in.

"What is it you want, humble and very, very simple peasant?" Frances asked. "Lady Freckles and I are occupied."

"Your presence is required in the Ball Room, your Royal Highnesses." Mr Greenwood rose to his feet again, and then kowtowed a few times for good measure.

"It is our pleasure to attend at once," Frances declared gravely, and Amy bit on her lip, so as not to burst out laughing.

They shuffled into the hallway, following Mr Greenwood awkwardly in their ridiculously oversized shoes.

He glanced at their feet and observed, "You might not break your necks if you were to take those off and put on your regular shoes. Just an idea."

Amy secretly agreed, holding out her arms sideways and swinging them a little to keep her balance, but Frances wasn't having it. "I like these," she told her father. "They are elegant."

Mr Greenwood snorted. "Elegant indeed."

One of the women volunteers —Amy thought it might be Tamara but she wasn't sure of all the names yet— emerged from the doorway Mr Greenwood was heading to.

"I've told you before, Tom," she scolded Mr Greenwood. "Women and shoes. Don't intervene. Just don't."

Frances and Amy laughed so hard and loud that they both nearly fell over, and swayed all over the place for a moment before they held on to each other, and somehow regained their balance.

"Fine," Mr Greenwood grumbled. "Not my necks. Your necks. If you insist on breaking them…" He shrugged helplessly, then departed from the hallway.

"Puh!" Frances said, and then shuffled into the next room with as much dignity as she could muster. Amy imitated her, doing her best to put on an outward show of confidence. She had no idea how people actually walked in high heels without falling over, and recalled instances of seeing women, and sometimes men on St James Street, gracefully gliding by on high heels as if it walking in them was the simplest thing in the world.

The new room was an office of sorts, with three desks tucked away in various corners. All were overflowing with papers, ledgers, books and other items. Daylight fell in through the windows. Instead of unsorted piles of donated goods, there were plastic crates piled up in the middle of the room, many of them with open lids, labelled 'gloves', 'socks', 'hoodies', 'wool hats', 'towels', and 'toiletries'.

Mr Greenwood walked towards the furthest desk and sat down, to frown at a computer screen. The walls behind him were hidden by notice boards from which hung a multitude of post-it notes, held in place by magnets, and on which numerous names and telephone numbers had been written. It looked like he had swept part of the clutter on his desk in an even untidier pile, to make place for a few of the in-flight meal boxes.

Amy tried not to gawp at the desk, as she made a mental comparison with her father's rigidly neat desk. He'd have a fit if he saw this desk! She giggled at the thought.

"Why did you summon us, oh commonest of common persons?" Frances put on her regal airs again.

"Did I?" Mr Greenwood tore his eyes away from the computer screen, and looked genuinely puzzled for a moment. "Doesn't matter, I just got an offer for a shed load of bicycles, we'll have to collect though. Van is mostly empty anyway, for a change. I'll see if tomorrow morning suits..." He glanced back at the computer screen, and his fingers flurried over the keyboard. He hailed someone passing behind Amy and Frances. "Big John!"

Amy turned to look to see Big John passing by, carrying a bulging bin bag.

"Aye, Tom?" Big John asked.

"You said you'd be in tomorrow, right? Can you be in by..." Mr Greenwood checked his computer screen, "...nine? We got an interesting collection in Worthing, but a limited window of opportunity."

"Will do, Boss," Big John answered, before stepping out of the office space.

"Sweet," Mr Greenwood said with satisfaction in his voice, before rapidly tapping on his keyboard.

"Dad!" Frances exclaimed. "You said you wanted us here."

"Oh?" Mr Greenwood looked at her, furrowing his brow as if trying to recall.

"This is why I am going to need therapy later," Frances confided to Amy, before turning back to her father. "*Expensive* therapy, Dad. You could save us a fortune, you know."

There was a loud beep in a little corridor to their side which served as a rudimentary kitchen. Amy could see an electric kettle and boxes full of tea bags and sugar, next to a microwave which was blinking a little red light at them.

"Ah yes!" Mr Greenwood exclaimed. He got off his chair and walked towards the corridor, talking all the while. "Since you two worked so hard unloading the in-flights, I thought we'd all have a little taste."

Frances grabbed one of the in-flight meal boxes on the desk and peered at the writing. She frowned. "Dad, I don't think you're supposed to stick these in the microwave."

"Well the oven is broken," Mr Greenwood replied. "So I figured if I took the food out of the tin-foil tray, a microwave would work just as well."

He opened the microwave door and peered inside, pursing his lips.

"They add *to-use* instructions for a *reason*, Dad." Frances shook her head warily, the multi-coloured metallic strips of her party wig swaying along merrily. She walked towards the kitchen corridor and Amy followed.

Mr Greenwood retrieved a plate from the microwave. "Ouch!" He yelped, and threw the plate onto the counter, adding an unnecessary explanation: "Hot!"

They all stared at the plate. It contained one of the twelve-thousand in-flight breakfasts, and looked anything but appetizing. The beans had all cracked into small segments, the tomato sauce congealed into a blob of red goo. There was bacon that looked more like greasy strips of fat, quivering like jelly from the transfer of the plate from microwave to kitchen counter. The scrambled eggs had turned runny, the pale yellow liquid slowly spreading around the plate. A sausage had been ripped into two halves, the edges outward and jagged, suggesting a small explosion of sorts.

Frances began to laugh. Mr Greenwood picked up a sausage half. He peered inside the hard skin, which didn't yield at all to the pressure of his fingers.

"It's empty," Mr Greenwood said in wonder. "Nothing inside at all." He looked at the plate again, as did Amy, trying to discern where the contents of the sausage might have gone.

"Not a sausage," Amy quipped.

Mr Greenwood laughed.

"What's the use-by date?" Frances asked.

Mr Greenwood shook his head. "Still okay for a couple of weeks. Prolly better if we take a few meals home and try them in the oven."

"I told you so," Frances declared with satisfaction.

"Meow?" A cat appeared, a big tabby tom cat, with an unsymmetrical face and broad scarred nose which lent it a particularly evil look. Amy was immediately smitten, she loved cats but her father was allergic, so they couldn't have any animals at home.

"Ah, General," Mr Greenwood greeted the cat. "Perfect timing as usual, you furry scrounger." He picked up the plate from the counter and set in front of General.

General approached the plate warily and cautiously sniffed its contents. His eyes seemed to widen, he uttered an aggrieved "Meow", raised his tail straight in the air, and stalked away, clearly offended.

Mr Greenwood, Frances and Amy all burst into laughter.

There would be more laughter that afternoon. Amy helped Frances to shift through some of the bags in the big central room, sorting out potentially useful items in various plastic boxes supplied by Big John. They worked hard, but it didn't really feel like work. Frances had switched on an old transistor radio, and they sang along with the songs they liked, and dissed the ones they didn't. Time flew by unnoticed, until Mr Greenwood joined them to announce it was time to give Amy a lift home.

"Aww," Amy said, and pouted in an exaggerated fashion.

"You can come back," Frances consoled her.

"Anytime," Mr Greenwood added.

Amy smiled. That was a prospect she looked forward to a great deal because, Amy registered with sudden surprise, she hadn't been this happy for a long time.

6. The Ice Rink at Pavilion Parade

School was out. Amy and Frances lingered inside the school library. Mr Greenwood was away on some errand in Hastings, so Frances had some time on her hands. She proposed going into town. Amy liked that idea, and sent her dad a text to tell him she'd be spending some time with Frances before coming home.

"Right," Amy said, as she put her phone away. "Let's go!"

She started walking, but stopped when Frances didn't follow.

"Shouldn't we wait for your dad to answer?" Frances asked.

Amy laughed. "Then we could be stuck here for hours. He doesn't notice much except his work when he's in his office. He might answer later, but I don't think he'll mind. He didn't the other day, did he?"

"And your mum?"

"She'll be at work until six, and then she has to get Jacob from the nursery. She's usually home about half six."

"Ah, so you're off-radar for a few hours."

"Yup," Amy confirmed with a smile.

They counted their money. They had enough for two single bus tickets, so they opted to walk down to town now, and catch a bus back up later.

Their first stop was the Open Market. They browsed in a few of the shops, trying on colourful shawls in one, playing with dragon hand-puppets in another, and having laughs modelling a variety of headwear.

After that, they drifted toward the seafront, but stopped when they reached the Royal Pavilion. Frances indicated the ice rink in front of the Pavilion's domes and minarets.

"I need the loo," she said, "and then we can watch the skaters from the café."

"I didn't know you could just go in?"

"Well, I've never asked." Frances grinned. "I just walk around like I belong there. And they've got clean loos."

They circled back to the towering and domed North Gate, because the approach to the ice rink was through the Pavilion Gardens. Amy always loved it there. She was as proud of the Pavilion as she was fond of Brighton's seagulls. There was Palace Pier of course, and the pier was special, but other seaside towns had piers too, and none had Brighton's Royal Pavilion.

It was even more magical when the ice rink was up. The interior of the café erected in front of the main Pavilion building was warm and bright, made merry by many Christmas decorations and lights. The short limb of the low L-shaped building was a hive of cheerful activity, with people changing their shoes for skates, preparing to go out onto the ice between the café and the Pavilion's front façade.

When Frances emerged from the loo, the girls went out on the terrace in front of the café, just as a new shift of skaters moved onto the ice. The girls leaned on the wooden railing, taking in the spectacle.

Loud music played, and whenever the terrace doors were opened and shut, the murmur of conversation and laughter would drift out of the café. The Pavilion's façade was spectacular in detail and magical to boot, as the walls, domes and minarets were lit up, the colours slowly blending from blue to purple to pink.

The centre of the ice was dominated by skaters displaying their skills with flair, swerving and spinning about in a blur. The majority were circling the rink at various speeds; talking, laughing, and smiling. The outer edge was claimed by those who moved forwards in a clumsy and ungainly manner, their faces grimly concentrated, or else in the throes of a panic, as they held on to the railing for dear life, their legs flailing about wildly beneath them.

Every now and then, Amy and Frances would have to stand back, clearing the railing for the few would-be skaters who had simply given up moving their legs altogether, and were hauling themselves along the railing using their arms. One such passer-by, a pot-bellied, bulking man, had an expression which suggested he was on a life or death mission. He was clearly determined to stay on the ice, because they had seen him pass once or twice before, but it was more a matter of desperate determination than enjoyment.

At least he's trying, Amy thought.

One of the central skaters burst out of a spin and sailed over the ice with the grace of a dancer, coming to a halt next to the bulking man. It was a teenage girl, her face animated by pure joy.

"Isn't this FUN?!" She asked the bulking man.

He forced a smile, after which he said between clenched teeth, "Fantastic."

Amy and Frances exchanged a grin.

"Come on!" The girl stretched out her hand in invitation. "I'll take you for a spin."

"NOOO!!" The man replied, tightening his grip on the railing. "I'll, er, make it in my own time. You go on, enjoy yourself, have a good time."

"Always!" The girl burst into movement, instantly a blur again as she sped into the circling traffic, weaving by slower skaters.

The man groaned and reached out his arms to pull himself further along the railing.

Grinning broadly, Amy and Frances took their place by the railing again.

"That would have been my dad," Amy indicated the bulking man's slow progress.

"Mine's a better skater then," Frances said. "He took me here last weekend, and he wasn't half bad, but I still got in three laps to his one!"

Amy thought of the hectic busyness at Mr Greenwood's office. "Does he have time for skating?"

"Not really." Frances shook her head. "But he makes a point of making some time now and then, just for the two of us."

"That's nice," Amy said, her eyes on the changing colours of the Pavilion's central dome.

"Do your parents make time?"

Amy shook her head.

They used to. She had happy memories of expeditions to the seafront, the Open Market, North Laine, the Lanes, Kemptown, and other places around town, or the Devil's Dyke and Ditchling Beacon on the Downs on sunny weekends. Then Gran had got ill, a cancer which took a year to...to suck all the life out of her, and family life had revolved around visits and care. After that, Mum's pregnancy and the arrival of Jacob had dominated the Wheatley household.

She immediately felt guilty, when an image of Hailey drifted into her mind. Amy had a lot compared to Hailey, at least.

"I'm sorry," Frances said.

"I've got a home. It isn't so bad." Amy shrugged. She recalled Hailey's pained reaction to the mention of family, and added, "And it's safe."

They stepped back, as a gaggle of giggling girls skated towards the railing and slammed into it. Two of them fell on the ice and had to be helped up, before the group continued on its merry way.

Amy and Frances stepped back to the railing. Frances said: "Safe is good, a lot of people don't even have that."

"I just don't understand why people are living on the streets," Amy said. "People like Hailey." Amy had already told Frances about her encounter with Hailey, although she had left out the startling extent of her mother's anger. "I thought people like that would get help. Mum said that Hailey could have got help if she wanted to, and chose to live on the street instead."

Frances took a deep breath. "Seriously, I haven't met a single homeless person who actually chooses to live on the streets. If they are not from Brighton, they are told they have to go back home and ask for help there."

"But she said home wasn't safe."

"Do you believe her?" Frances asked.

Amy recalled the haunted look in Hailey's eyes, when she had rocked to and fro, repeating that home wasn't safe. "Yes, I do. No doubt about it."

"There are many more like that," Frances said. "More than two hundred people in Brighton living on the streets. And then all the people living in cars and caravans. There're thousands of them, but they aren't counted."

Amy looked around her; the fairy-tale setting was an odd place to be having this conversation. Everything seemed so carefree...but there was a whole other Brighton out there, much of it unpleasant and mostly invisible.

"You know so much about this!" She told Frances.

"It's Dad's work, isn't it? His real job is running an online mail order firm, some of The Office storage space is used for that. But he spends most of his time helping people out."

"I think that's amazing!"

Frances smiled. "So do I. That's why I help out, just about every school day, and on weekends too. I don't really mind all the sorting and stuff. Just don't tell Dad I said that. I like giving him a hard time about it."

Amy gave Frances a thumbs-up, but her mind turned to the thousands of people Frances spoke about, living in Brighton, but not in a home. She felt a stab of bitterness. "If the problem is really that big, then my parents lied to me about it. They said that the Council was taking care of it. I can't believe they lied to me."

Frances shook her head. "I don't think so, Amy. I think your parents were just fooled. Dad says that the Council plays with the numbers to hide the problem. They give the TV-people and the newspaper reporters the wrong information."

"Aren't reporters supposed to check and find out if it's true?"

Frances shrugged. "Maybe in the movies or on telly, I don't think they do a lot of that in real life anymore."

Amy was relieved to learn that her parents might have been fooled. It was better than pretending a real problem didn't exist. She was puzzled, however, by what Frances had said about the Council. Amy didn't really know much about the City Council at all, but she had always vaguely assumed they were there to help people. She asked: "But why do they do all that? Don't they want to help?"

"Money. I think it's all about money," Frances said.

"It's cruel."

"It's cruel," Frances confirmed. "Cruel and bloody unfair, that's what I think."

They stepped back from the railing. The bulking man was passing again, his face rigid with concentration, beads of sweat on his forehead. He didn't seem to notice them, or anybody else at all, seemingly intent only on surviving his ordeal.

"So why does your dad do it?" Amy asked. "Help people the way he does?"

Frances rolled her eyes. "Just don't ever ask him that when I'm around, I've heard the story like a million times."

"Fair enough, but can you tell me?"

"When he first came to Brighton from up north, like ages before I was born, he was homeless himself. He slept under an upturned boat on the beach, got himself into a lot of trouble. Then someone offered him a helping hand, got him out of the mess he was in. That's the short version."

"So then he wanted to help others in turn?"

"Yeah." Frances nodded. "That's what it boils down to." She retrieved her mobile phone from her coat pocket, and glanced at the screen. "Do you want to go visit Hailey? We've got just about enough time."

"Visit Hailey?"

"Yeah, why not? I reckon I know where she'll be at this time of day."

Amy furrowed her brow. Mum had specifically said, a number of times, that Amy wasn't to hang around homeless people. To visit Hailey after that warning was a big thing. It wasn't that Amy had never been disobedient before, but she recognised that most of that was mischief. To defy her parents' wishes in this was whole other matter.

A couple of seagulls sailed by overhead, heading towards the seafront, screeching piratical laughter that could be heard even over the loud music.

Pirates and smugglers.

Gran had once told her that Sussex folk all hailed from pirates and smugglers. "Stubborn as can be," Gran had said, and then chuckled. "There's none more stubborn than folk from Sussex, 'we wunt be druv' is our motto."

I'm not supposed to. But I want to. If only to apologize for Mum's outburst.

"Well?" Frances asked.

We wunt be druv.

Amy nodded. "I'd like that very much," she said. "Lead the way."

7. In the Shadow of St Bart's at Providence Place

They found Hailey in front of St Bartholomew's Church. The tall dark-red brick church dwarfed the buildings around it. Its front façade towered over a tiny park, not much more than a path curving through a few patches of grass beneath a handful of trees. There was a wooden sculpture at the end of the mini park, curved beams rising from the ground like the ribs of a shipwrecked boat. A long wall at the end of the park bore giant white-edged, black letters: BORN AND BRED.

Hailey was sitting on one of the benches lining the path, but she wasn't alone. Her face was turned to a man sitting next to her. The man had a wild nest of grey-streaked black hair. He wore a rumpled black suit, complete with tie, and a big smudged green parka coat. Two other men were sitting on the next bench, one a hulking figure, imposingly tall even when sitting down, dressed entirely in jungle camouflage outdoor gear.

Amy stalled. Hailey had been different somehow, but she was wary of strangers, and she didn't know these three men. The park, which had seemed a pleasant oasis of peace just a moment ago, now seemed ominously deserted other than the four on the benches. She hissed: "Frances!"

Just then, the man sitting next to the hulking green man raised his arm and waved enthusiastically. "Frances!" He called out. "Amy!"

Amy hadn't really taken him in, as her attention had been drawn to the sheer size of the large green man next to him. Now that she looked at him, she recognised him from The Office. "Big John!" She exclaimed.

Big John grinned, and the girls walked closer.

The huge green man looked at Amy, and slowly shook his head. "That is Big John," he drawled solemnly in a deep voice, as he pointed at his much smaller companion. Then he pointed his finger towards his own chest, "I am Little John."

He guffawed loudly, and the whole bench seemed to shake with his laughter.

"Dad made that up." Frances told Amy.

"He needed to tell us apart," Big John explained.

"I am Little John," Little John said slowly, and then roared with laughter again.

"Which was sensible," Frances said. "But then, of course, Dad messed it all up by calling big John Little John, and little John Big John." She lifted her eyes to the sky with exasperation written on her face. "Confusion all around."

"No," Little John looked alarmed. "I like it, it's funny."

"I was just joking, Little John," Frances said quickly. "It's alright."

"Alright?" Little John looked at her with concern written on his broad face, his eyes pleading. "I want to keep my name. I like it."

"And you will, mate," Big John reached up to pat Little John on his shoulder. He spoke to the big man like he was a very young child. "Like Frances says, it's alright, mate, everything is going to be alright. You are Little John and you will stay Little John."

"Little!" Little John exclaimed, his mood instantly lifted. He began to chuckle. "Little, that's what I am."

"Exactly," Frances said, and gave him a thumbs-up, which the big man returned with both of his huge hands and a broad grin. The sheer pleasure on his face was contagious, and Amy grinned along with him.

Frances turned to Big John. "We came to see Hailey."

Big John nodded. "Bless you Frances. Hailey ain't having the best of days."

Amy and Frances turned to Hailey.

"Hailey?" Amy asked.

Hailey turned her head slowly, to face the girls. Amy could see that Hailey's bruise was beginning to fade, and she had a plaster over the cuts on her forehead. She looked clean too, her red hair gleaming and her skin clear of smudges of dirt, but her eyes were red rimmed, and there was none of the hard mask, just an expression of despair, and tear drops rolling slowly down wet cheeks.

Frances stepped forward, and dropped on her knees in front of Hailey, taking one of the woman's hands in both her own. "Oh Hailey! What's happened?"

Hailey's hand tightened around Frances's. The young woman quickly wiped her cheeks with the sleeve of her free arm. She looked at the man sitting next to her, a silent plea for help in her eyes.

"Hi Gaz," Frances said. "What's happened?"

"Hey Frances," the black-haired man answered with a short, sad smile.

Amy saw that Gaz had remarkably bright blue eyes, brimming with sharp intelligence. His face was gaunt and clean shaven, his expression one of sorrow.

"They took our stuff," Gaz said.

"Bastards!" Frances fumed.

"What?" Amy asked. "Who?"

"Council bin men," Big John stepped up next to Amy. "Just about two hours ago."

"We went to First Base this morning," Gaz explained. He spoke slowly, but not in the manner in which Little John spoke slowly, it was rather as if Gaz was weighing up each word, before speaking it out loud. "For a shower, and some breakfast."

"I took your advice," Hailey said directly to Amy, the first sign that she recognized Amy, who was pleasantly surprised by the acknowledgement. "Shower. Did feel better." Hailey shrugged. "For a bit anyway, until we got back."

"What happened when you got back?" Amy asked.

"We caught the bin men red-handed, piling up our gear into their lorry." Gaz said. "We'd stashed it out of sight, it wasn't a bother for anyone."

"Yours too?" Frances asked Big John, who shook his head in reply.

"Just mine and Hailey's. This time," Gaz said. He sighed. "Everything but our day packs, which we'd brought along to First Base. All my books are gone. You know how I like to read when it's daylight."

"That bivvy bag your old man gave me was really warm," Hailey said, her lips trembling. "I felt so good after that shower, almost human, then this happens."

"But they can't do that!?!" Amy exclaimed. "Just take your belongings like that!"

"Well," Big John said. "Council tells the media they don't do such things. So it really didn't happen."

"Didn't happen...?" Amy was confused.

"Not officially, but they do it all the time anyway," Gaz explained. "I talked with the bin men, tried to persuade them to give us a break. They were feeling bad about it, they really were. They said they had very strict instructions from above, wouldn't say who."

"I begged the bastards," Hailey said, a flash of that hard mask of hers briefly appearing on her face. She spat on the ground.

"They're afraid," Big John said.

"Afraid of what?" Amy asked.

"Losing their jobs," Gaz said. "They encounter the likes of us often enough to know what would happen to them if they lost their income. Most people are only a few steps away from having to make do on a park bench. Just a couple of pay checks."

"No excuse," Frances said. "People shouldn't do what they know is wrong."

"It's a bit more complicated than…" Gaz began.

"No it's not," Frances said firmly. "If everybody simply refused to do what is obviously wrong, it would stop."

"True," Big John agreed. "Unlikely to happen, but true."

"Can't you get your things back?" Amy asked.

Hailey barked a bitter laugh.

"Yes," Gaz said. "They said it would be stored at some kind of lost & found depot for a few weeks, and gave us the address. We'd have to pay a twenty-five quid fine though, or they won't return our stuff."

"Each," Hailey added. She began to cry, and pressed her face against Gaz's shoulder.

Gaz folded an arm around Hailey's shoulders. He looked at Amy with an apology written on his face. "We didn't have much, none of it worth fifty quid, but when you've barely got anything at all…"

Amy nodded her understanding, her emotions surging between disbelief and anger, and a little bit of guilt…if Hailey hadn't gone to have a shower, as Amy had suggested, maybe she wouldn't have lost her stuff.

"Fifty quid!" Frances exclaimed. "How on earth do they expect you to find fifty quid?"

"I tried calling Tom," Big John told her. "But he wasn't answering his phone."

"Dad'll be dead busy then, or driving," Frances said. "But he always answers me."

She released Hailey's hand and scrambled to her feet, retrieving her mobile from a coat pocket. "Don't worry Hailey, we're gonna sort you out."

"She was too ashamed to ask," Gaz told Frances.

"It's no problem, really it isn't," Frances said to Hailey. "Dad'll know you didn't lose those things on purpose."

She turned on the speaker, and they listened to the ringing tone for what seemed an awfully long time.

"My delightful offspring," Mr Greenwood's voice sounded at last. "Make it quick, I'm on the A27, heading back to Brighton. I've had to pull over."

"Dad, I'm with Hailey and Gaz at St Bart's. The bin men took all their stuff."

Mr Greenwood cursed, using colourful expletives.

"Very educational, Dad," Frances said dryly. "Can we help them out?"

"Van's empty." Mr Greenwood replied. "I took six thousand in-flights to the food bank people in Hastings, and they were short of everything else too, so I unloaded everything I had. I'm getting close to the Amex stadium. I'll head straight for The Office, load up gear for two, and come straight down to...St Bart's you said?"

"The little park in front of the church," Frances confirmed.

"I'll be there within the hour then. Tell Gaz and Hailey to stay put. You too, I'll give you a ride home. Over and out."

"Over and out," Frances answered. She put away her phone and told Gaz and Hailey: "We'll have you properly kitted out before dark."

"Much obliged," Gaz said. "Truly. Nights have been turning damn cold lately."

"Bless," Hailey smiled at Frances through her tears. "You're an angel."

Amy stared at Frances, awed at the manner in which her friend had taken control of the situation. Frances was younger than Amy, only eleven-point-two-five, but at that moment she seemed much older and wiser.

Big John addressed Frances: "Right, since you've got this sorted, I should be off to the Open Market before it shuts. The Streets Café will do us a cuppa, and might throw in a bacon butty for Little John, they've taken a liking to him."

"Hungry," Little John added, rubbing his belly, which growled with anticipation.

"See you at the Clock Tower on Sunday?" Frances asked Big John.

"Yes, the Clock Tower, definitely," He smiled. "Come on Little John, let's go."

"Go where?" Little John looked puzzled.

"We're going to get some food," Big John answered.

"Food! I'm hungry!" Little John's face lit up, and he rose to his feet, towering over all of them, before shuffling off after Big John.

Frances turned to Amy. "If I ask my Dad to drop you off, we've got that bus money to spend, don't we?"

Amy nodded. "Will I be back in Fiveways on time?"

"Time to spare," Frances promised. "Gaz, Hailey. We'll get you a cuppa. Coffee or tea?

"You don't have..." Hailey began.

"Nonsense, a cuppa will do you good Hailey," Gaz said. "Cup of tea would be marvellous Frances. We'll be here when you get back."

"In a jiffy," Frances promised, and looked at Amy. "Coming?"

8. Devising a Plot on Ann Street

When Amy and Frances turned the corner onto Ann Street, they saw both Johns ambling towards the flow of people on London Road.

"Little John is really tall, isn't he?" Amy marvelled.

Frances didn't answer. Instead, she cast a look behind her to make sure they were out of sight, and then stopped walking. To Amy's alarm, her friend buried her face in her hands, after which her shoulders shook and she let out a distraught sob.

"Frances?!"

Amy's friend looked up again, and wiped a sleeve over her eyes. "It's just so bloody unfair!"

"Totally unfair," Amy agreed. "But I thought...you were...just now in the park..."

"Gotta keep smiling, for their sake. Someone's gotta smile," Frances said. She closed her eyes, and took a deep breath.

Amy wondered if that was something Mr Greenwood had taught her, it seemed like something he would say.

"But you know, Amy," Frances said, opening her eyes again. "You never get used to it. It's hard enough for them to just survive. But it's even more unfair when stuff like this happens. There is no need to make their life more horrible than it already is. It just makes me want to kick somebody..."

"...But you have to smile."

"You saw Hailey, she was already really upset..."

Frances's lower lip began to tremble. Amy stepped closer and gave her friend a hug. Frances returned it, holding on tight. She shook a few more times, making that sobbing sound.

"You did really well," Amy said softly. "Back in the park, I was amazed..."

They let go of each other, and Frances stepped back, wiping her eyes with her sleeve again. "When you get to know them, they're just ordinary people, normal people, like you and me..."

"I am beginning to get that," Amy said.

"I know." Frances smiled. It was a sad smile, but Amy was relieved to see something other than anguish on her friend's face. "It's good to be able to share it. Thanks for that, you're a good mate, Amy. I'm glad we met."

"Me too," Amy said. "I want to help, I just don't know how..."

Frances's face brightened. "Why don't you come to the Clock Tower, on Sunday? We can always use a few extra hands. We start at quarter to one."

"What's on at the Clock Tower?"

"We do a street kitchen, every Sunday. Dad organises it, but loads of people come and pitch in."

"A street kitchen?" Amy thought about all the tins of soup she had seen at The Office. "Soup?"

"Not just soup," Frances said. "There's usually a stew, or pasta, and some meat as well. And tea and coffee. We serve it to homeless people, or anybody who's hungry and doesn't have food. There's dozens of them who come, no, more than that even! And there's like a mini-market, with useful things they can take if they want. Oh, you should come Amy, it's always fun, but it'll be more fun if you're there."

Frances's enthusiasm was infectious at first. Amy wanted nothing more than to go help out at this street kitchen, but then her spirits sank. Mum would have had a fit if she had seen Amy in the little park just now, visiting Hailey and other homeless people. How much worse would that be if Amy went to meet and feed a small army of them?

"I want to come, Frances..."

"Yeet!"

"But...my mum and dad...they don't want me to hang around..."

"You won't be," Frances said. "You'll be hanging around me. And my dad will be there as well."

Amy shrugged. She didn't think Mum would see it that way.

"Ask them if you can spend the day with me on Sunday," Frances suggested. "Just don't tell them where. Everybody hangs out with their friends some time, it's perfectly normal."

Amy understood the logic of that, but she'd still be hoodwinking her parents, big time. "I'll think about it, okay? I need some time to think."

Frances was about to protest, but then thought better of it. "Okay, sorry, I didn't mean to push you or anything."

"No, no!" Amy shook her head. "I want to come, I truly do. It's just that..."

"I understand," Frances said. "Just think about it. Now, we'd better go get that tea, before they start to worry about us."

"Good idea," Amy agreed, and the girls walked down Ann Street to join the throngs crowding London Road.

9. Fiveways Wilf

Amy spent most of Saturday morning in her room. Frances was away, Mr Greenwood had taken her out of Brighton for the day to visit family.

Even though Amy had only known Frances for a couple of days, she felt her friend's absence keenly, and was at a loss what to do. Amy tried to lose herself in her sketches and drawings, something she usually succeeded in for hours on end, but her heart simply wasn't in it this time.

It had been an eventful week. Amy's mind endlessly replayed her first meeting with Hailey, Mum's furious reaction, escaping from the Year Nine girls with only moments to spare, laughter in The Office, revelations at the ice rink, and drama at St Bart's.

All the time, she struggled with Mum's clear instructions about homeless people, and her own intense longing to be at the Clock Tower on Sunday. Whatever else, it seemed that whenever Mr Greenwood was around, people were being helped. Wasn't it far better to be doing something, rather than just stand around feeling helpless?

When Mum called Amy down for lunch, Amy went down in trepidation, her belly aflutter, not sure if she'd have the courage to raise the subject.

"How was your morning?" Mum asked Dad, who had gone into town to return some books to the Jubilee Library.

"Pleasant enough," Dad answered, between bites of his sandwich. "Went to the Jubilee. Ambled around North Laine for a bit. Mind you, had a bit of a fright."

Amy only half-listened, chewing on her bread robotically without deriving any pleasure from it, her head still in a mental swirl.

"How so?" Mum asked.

"I got off the bus on North Street and headed for the library," Dad said. "Bought a roll because I was feeling a bit peckish. I was munching on it as I strolled down New Road. Then all of a sudden a beggar stumbles up to me, starts rambling on about how great a roll is when you're hungry."

"Unbelievable!" Mum remarked.

"I've kind of got used to it," Dad said. "It's become near impossible to walk through the city centre without being accosted for spare change, a cigarette, or whatnot. The thing is, this chap was massive, easily six feet ten, I reckon, built like a bull. Dressed in army gear like he was about to go off to a war somewhere."

LITTLE JOHN!! Amy quickly took another bite of her sandwich, and tried to keep her expression neutral.

"Did he threaten you?" Mum asked.

"Not really," Dad answered. "He kept on talking about the kind of rolls and sandwiches he liked to eat, but his size was intimidating, and you just never know, do you?"

"They are unpredictable," Mum said.

Amy struggled to keep her mouth shut. From what she had seen of Little John, the big man had probably just been trying to be friendly, but there was no way she could tell her parents that. They would want to know why Amy knew Little John, and the 'what', 'where', and 'how' of it.

"I've said it before, and I'll say it again," Mum said, with a sideway glance at Amy. "It's an absolute disgrace that all these beggars are allowed to harass decent people. Don't we have a right to feel safe on the streets?"

"What if this man was just hungry, or lonely?" Amy asked, unable to say nothing at all. "Is it so wrong to give food to someone who is hungry?"

"It's not our responsibility," Mum answered. "And it shouldn't be. We've told you this before. We pay our taxes, and enough of that money goes to all sorts of programmes to help these people."

"If they refuse that help," Dad added. "That is their choice, isn't it? Nobody is making them stay on the streets."

"But..." Amy started saying.

"It's not our responsibility," Mum repeated. "The ones who refuse help do so because they'd rather have their..." She paused, looking at Dad.

"She's old enough to know," Dad said. "Listen sweetheart, some people get addicted to alcohol, or drugs. They don't want to kick that habit, but that's what they have to do if they want to get accepted into programmes to get them back into housing, back into a normal life. When they make that choice, to get drunk, or buy drugs, then the rest is their responsibility. They could have spent that money on other things, like rent, or clean clothes."

Mum added: "Or else they make far more money begging on the street than they would if they applied for benefits, or found a job."

"You make it sound like people want to live on the streets," Amy protested.

"Well, many of them do," Mum said in a curt tone, a signal that she was tiring of the topic. "And those that don't are helped off the streets by the Council."

"How do you know?" Amy made a last attempt to try and change her parents' minds.

"Sweetheart," Dad said. "I understand that you're concerned. Anybody would be, but there is more to it than that which meets the eye. *The Argus* runs regular articles on the beggar problems in the city, and all the people who work with the street folk insist that it's wrong to give them money, or food and drink."

Not all people, Amy thought. *Mr Greenwood works with them too. And Frances said she knew nobody at all who actually wants to live on the streets.*

"Now," Mum said. "I'd really appreciate it if we could finish our lunch in peace. Let's talk about something more cheerful. It'll be Christmas soon, when should we put the tree up? We'll have so much fun putting up the decorations, won't we?"

"I suppose so," Amy said, staring at her plate. She had always liked decorating the Christmas tree. This year, though, Amy wasn't sure. To her, Christmas had always been about warmth and goodwill, caring and sharing, but she'd never fully realised that this only applied to some and excluded others.

When she helped her mother clear up after lunch, Mum asked her to pop up to the Fiveways shops.

"I completely forgot to get some eggs, and we could use an extra pint of milk as well."

Amy was happy to go on the errand, she felt a sudden urge to get out of the house, it felt stifling. She meandered up the streets slowly, being in no hurry to return home.

She had plenty to think about. Amy had hoped to broach a Sunday visit to Frances during lunch, but that plan had been derailed by the extent of her parents' resistance to the notion of helping homeless people. It seemed that Frances's suggestion to not mention exactly where they would be, or what they would be doing, was the best option.

Amy sat down on a low front garden wall, swinging her legs.

This wasn't a matter of a small, convenient fib. It wasn't an outright lie either, because she'd just be leaving some information out.

But what if Mum and Dad want to know exactly where I'll be? And what I'll be doing?

That would mean fabricating something, and that was a big lie. On the other hand, spending the whole Sunday at home, with nothing but her thoughts for company, unable to escape into drawing or reading...Amy shivered.

She was distracted from her thoughts when she suddenly noticed a movement by her feet. It was a cat, a beautiful ginger Persian, its short nose and round face suggested a nonchalant disdain, though it was eyeing Amy with what appeared to her to be a thoughtful look, looking as distinguished as an old-fashioned gentleman.

"Wilf!" Amy said.

Everybody who lived in Fiveways knew Wilf. The ginger Persian made a habit of wandering about the area, visiting the shops at Fiveways, sometimes for hours on end. Amy had seen him from a distance before, but never this close up.

Wilf hopped onto the wall and sat down next to Amy. He looked at her expectantly, and then raised his chin in invitation. When Amy scratched it, Wilf began to purr loudly. It was a deep bass sound, like he was humming.

"Oh Wilf," Amy said. "Aren't you a beautiful cat?"

Wilf purred his agreement, shifting his head so that Amy could scratch his lower chin.

"Betcha you're not walking around having to make a difficult decision," Amy told the cat. She began to stroke Wilf's head and back, marvelling at how soft and downy his fur was. Wilf continued purring as she petted him. Amy began to feel calmer, her thoughts slowing down. For a blissful moment, it seemed that her entire universe shrunk to the garden wall, herself, and the purring ginger cat. It was a good feeling, and for the first time that day, Amy smiled.

"There you are!" A woman's voice tut-tutted. A strange voice Amy had never heard before. "I've been looking all over for you."

Who? Me?

Amy looked up in confusion, to see a woman, with short dark hair and a kind face, standing in front of her, hands on her hips, and shaking her head at Wilf.

Wilf looked at the woman, and then closed his eyes, nudging his head against Amy's hand to indicate he wanted another chin scratch.

"Are you Wilf's owner?" Amy asked the woman.

The woman laughed. "Wilf's really not one to be 'owned' - if anything, he owns me! Most people call 'Wilf's mum' and I'm sure Wilf sees me as 'Staff#1' but my actual name is Johanna."

Amy smiled at that, continuing to pet the cat, as Wilf seemed in no hurry to vacate the garden wall.

"I'm Amy," she said. "I've seen Wilf around before, but never this close. He's so soft!"

"He's adorable, and takes full advantage of that, don't you Wilf?"

Wilf ignored her.

"He also loves to get out and about," Johanna continued. "I thought he'd just potter around the garden this morning, but before long I started getting phone calls. Wilf's been seen here, seen there, seen everywhere. He even dropped by the Flour Pot Bakery as well as he loves to scrounge for food and hoover up dropped cake crumbs from under the tables."

Amy laughed, picturing Wilf strolling into the Flour Pot Bakery like it was the most normal thing in the world. "He's not very catlike is he? I mean, most cats I know are a bit stand-offish when they don't know people."

"Ah, I've found this with Persian cats," Johanna answered. "some of their character traits are a bit different from 'regular' cats. Wilf in particular; he's headstrong and I'm pretty sure he thinks he's a dog. He certainly chooses who he wishes to spend time and people feel honoured when he does!"

Wilf purred on.

"I've heard he visits all of the shops," Amy said.

"Almost all, and he also likes to catch a ride on buses. He'll walk right in with the other passengers and never bothers to buy a ticket."

Amy laughed. "Where does he catch a bus to?"

"To visit more people." Johanna sighed. "It's not always convenient, mind you, and some people assume I don't take good enough care of him, because he wanders around so much."

"Some people have silly opinions," Amy offered.

Johanna smiled at that. "Yes they do. Most people adore him, fortunately. They always tell me that he brings kindness and companionship. Sometimes Wilf seems to sense exactly who needs a bit of attention. He'll sit with them and make them smile and feel better. On the rare days that Wilf stays in, I get phone calls from people worried that they *haven't* seen him."

Amy smiled at that. "He made me smile and feel better. I think he knew I needed a bit of kindness."

Johanna looked at Amy appraisingly for a moment. "Yes, I think you are right. Life can be complicated sometimes, can't it?"

Amy responded with a heartfelt nod. "Do you think it's important, to be kind?"

"Kindness is just about the most important thing in life," Johanna said. "If we're not kind to each other, what do we have left? I like to think that Wilf's job is to remind us of that, when we're so busy that we forget it."

"I think you're right." Amy nodded. She liked Johanna. Even though the woman was oldish, at least over thirty, and therefore light years removed in age, she talked to Amy like a regular human being, instead of a child who couldn't possibly understand anything at all.

"Wilf was a rescue cat," Johanna said. "I'd like to think that maybe he remembers the help he got to find a home that loves and appreciates him and therefore understands that others need help sometimes too."

That remark made Amy think about what Frances had said about her father. Mr Greenwood had been a stray of sorts, rescued by someone helping him, and that someone had unwittingly inspired Mr Greenwood to go to great lengths to help others. "So maybe Wilf's kindness began with you? Because you took him in?"

Johanna laughed. "Well, I mustn't claim all the credit, it's in Wilf's character as well. But kindness helps a great deal. I work with rescue cats from time to time. You wouldn't believe the state of some of them, when they are brought in. Thin, dirty, matted, and crawling with fleas. It's amazing how they bounce back after a bit of kindness to become loving, purring companions."

"Like Wilf," Amy said, and scratched in between Wilf's ears.

"Like Wilf," Johanna agreed. "I reckon he does a grand job of teaching us to be kind, to think about others, and not just ourselves."

Wilf looked at his owner before dropping down from the wall. He walked over to Johanna and gave the woman's calves a gentle head butt.

"He's ready to go home now," Johanna said. "It was lovely meeting you Amy."

"And you! Wilf as well!"

"Will you be alright?" Johanna asked. "You're not lost are you?"

Amy shook her head. "I live just down the road, Mum sent me to the shops."

"That's good," Johanna smiled. "Goodbye then, until next time. Come on Wilf."

Johanna turned to go and Wilf followed her almost reluctantly with the resigned plod of a child brought in from playtime for his tea by his mum.

Amy watched them disappear, and then took out her phone to text Frances, for Amy had come to a decision. Kindness mattered above all else.

>*I'll ask parents 2night about Clock Tower 2morrow*<

Frances responded almost immediately.

>☺ ☺ ☺ *I talked 2 Dad he says 2 call him if they have questions*<

Frances added a phone number, before asking:

>*We can scoop U up at Fiveways shops. Half twelve*<

Amy answered:

>*I'll do my best. I'll let U know*<

That evening, toward the end of dinner, Amy finally gathered the courage to ask if she could spend the next day with Frances. Dad was quick to agree. Mum had questions. Who was Frances? Where did she live? Were her parents going to be there?

"I've never met these people before," Mum added, almost accusingly.

Amy looked at her father. "Dad?"

"What? Oh yes. I spoke to Frances's father earlier this week, Mr, eh?"

"Greenwood" Amy supplied.

"That's right," Dad said. "Mr Greenwood. He sounded alright to me, friendly chap."

"He said we could call him," Amy said. She quickly dialled the number, and laid the phone in the middle of the table, with the loudspeaker on. It was one way to avoid answering those specific questions Mum had asked.

"Tom Greenwood," Mr Greenwood answered.

"Mr Greenwood," Amy leant over the table to speak to the phone. "It's Amy. Amy Wheatley. You said it was alright for my parents to speak to you..."

"Indeed!" Mr Greenwood answered. "About tomorrow, am I right?"

Amy nodded, before realising Mr Greenwood couldn't possibly see that. "Yes, Mr Greenwood," she said, and leaned back again, hoping desperately that Mr Greenwood wouldn't give the game away. "I've put you on the speaker."

"Mr Greenwood," Mum said. "Nancy Wheatley here, Amy's mother."

"And Josh Wheatley," Dad added. "Amy's father, we spoke earlier this week."

"So we did," Mr Greenwood agreed. "Though I haven't had the pleasure of speaking with Amy's mother yet."

Mum nodded approvingly, and Amy dared a deep breath.

So far, so good.

"Mr Greenwood," Mum began, "Amy's asked us if she could spend the Sunday with your daughter."

"So I've been told," Mr Greenwood answered. "Though I really don't understand why she'd want to."

"Oh?" Mum was confused by that, as was Amy.

"I've got a catering job tomorrow," Mr Greenwood explained. "I'll be feeding a large number of people…"

Amy held her breath.

"…and I'll be expecting the girls to lend a helping hand," Mr Greenwood finished.

Frances's voice suddenly sounded loud and clear through the phone's speaker. "Dad, that's child labour!"

"Duly noted. Precisely, child labour," Mr Greenwood said. "Now I'm of the mind that a little work won't kill Frances."

"Yes it will!" Frances protested.

Mr Greenwood ignored her. "I rather reckon it's good for her. But, Mrs Wheatley, Mr Wheatley, I obviously can't speak for your daughter in this…"

"No, no," Dad said. "Marvellous, never too early to teach them a bit of responsibility, is it, Mr Greenwood?"

"I'll be keeping an eye on them," Mr Greenwood promised. "They won't be anywhere near the hot plates, or the hot drinks."

"That is good," Mum said.

Amy could hardly believe how well it was going, she could read her parents' faces well enough to see that they had been taken in by Mr Greenwood's charm, and liked what he was saying.

Mr Greenwood proposed: "I could pick Amy up at the Fiveways shops tomorrow at half twelve, and drop her back off home at five, or half-five?"

"That would be splendid, thank you Mr Greenwood," Mum said. "It's good to know she'll be in safe hands."

"Well that's arranged then." Mr Greenwood sounded satisfied. "Amy, be sure to give your parents my number, won't you? In case of emergencies. And I'd appreciate their phone numbers as well."

"I will, Mr Greenwood!"

"Excellent, we'll see you tomorrow then," Mr Greenwood said. "Good night, everyone."

The Wheatley's returned his goodbye, Amy with a smile on her face because she could barely believe that it had all been arranged with such ease. Her relief was mixed with delight at the prospect of spending her Sunday in Frances's company at the Clock Tower.

10. A Street Kitchen at the Clock Tower

Mr Greenwood's van was so loaded that it seemed to sag on its wheels when it shuddered to a halt in front of the Fiveways pub the next morning. Amy glanced in the back as she scrambled in to take a seat next to Frances. She couldn't even see the roof, because of all the boxes and other gear crammed in.

"Afternoon Amy," Mr Greenwood said, and then reached for the dashboard to pick up the black felt trilby hat from Aladdin's Cave. "You left this behind at The Office."

"That isn't mine," Amy said, placing her satchel by her feet and securing her seatbelt.

"Nonsense," Mr Greenwood answered. "You earned it fair and square, helping to unload all those in-flights."

"It looks good on you!" Frances took the hat from her father's hand and planted it on Amy's head.

"Thanks!" Amy beamed. She had rather liked the hat and it was a perfect fit. Wearing it, she felt like an intrepid explorer, and that was certainly apt, because Amy had the sense that she was embarking on a grand adventure when Mr Greenwood coaxed the van into movement.

As they headed down Ditchling Road into town, Amy chatted with Frances, but every now and then she would look out of the windows in wonder. She must have travelled this route a million times, without giving the familiar streets of Brighton a second thought, but this time everything seemed to be different. It was as if she was seeing the city for the first time.

It was already busy in the city centre, with heavy traffic and scores of people on the pavements, ambling along at leisure, or pacing in the pursuit of an errand. Amy wondered how many of them gave a second thought to the scattering of rough sleepers seated in shop doorways, huddled in their sleeping bags.

She spotted kids her own age, either in groups, or trailing parents. Only a week before, that might have been her, momentarily curious perhaps, as to the presence of homeless people on Brighton's streets, but otherwise blissfully unaware of what was going on.

When they arrived at the Clock Tower, Mr Greenwood parked the van on the pavement along Queen's Road. There were already people milling about. Amy recognised Tamara and Sue from The Office. Big John was there too, and he smiled a greeting when Amy and Frances clambered out of the van. Amy thought that they would start unloading the van straight away, but Mr Greenwood seemed in no rush. He wandered from person to person, to greet them and exchange a few words.

When he did finally open the van's rear doors, he started pulling at a folding table, which at first resisted his efforts to wedge it loose. Various people gathered behind him. They cheered when Mr Greenwood finally managed to wrestle the table from the tightly packed mass of items in the back of the van.

"Stop laughing at me and make yourself useful." Mr Greenwood grumbled at Big John and handed him the table.

"Aye, aye, Cap'n." Big John saluted before taking the table and walking to the semi-circular tier of stone seats facing the Clock Tower.

His place was taken by somebody else, and Amy was amazed at the industrious activity which followed. Mr Greenwood handed item after item to the volunteers, all of whom seemed to know exactly where to carry their loads, and did so in good cheer. As they bantered and joked, the open space between the stone seats and the Clock Tower, as well as the higher level of pavement behind the seats, were transformed in no time.

A row of folding tables were set up in front of the seats, and more placed on the raised pavement behind the seats. Amy helped place clear storage boxes on the upper level tables. There were boxes with gloves, scarves, socks, jumpers, jeans and coats. Some boxes held toiletries. One box was filled with new toothbrushes, another with tubes of toothpaste, and yet others with sanitary and hygiene products. Amy was particularly taken by a box of paperbacks, and she hoped Gaz would show up because he had lost his books and might be really pleased to find some new ones.

It was like a small market, drawing curious glances from passer-bys, and smiles from the first homeless people who began to gather around in growing numbers.

By the time they had finished setting up the improvised market stalls, the lower row of tables had been set up as well. There were piles of paper plates and cutlery, large steaming pans, platters of bread, tubs of butter, boxes of homemade cookies and regular biscuits, cakes and pasties donated by Greggs, and tall hot water dispensers surrounded by cups and tins filled with teabags, instant coffee, sugar, and cartons of milk.

Frances took Amy's hand and took her to a spot between the tables and the tier of seats.

"This is our table," she said proudly. Amy looked to see the bread and butter, a huge bag of shredded cheese, biscuits, cakes and pasties, as well as a pile of books and a box of CDs next to a charity collection box.

"We'll sell those for a fiver each," Frances pointed at the books and CDs. "Sometimes people who are just passing want to help out when they see what we're doing, so they can buy a book or CD."

Amy looked closer. The CDs were named "Musicians for Homeless", and the books were called *On Brighton Streets*, presented by something called Invisible Voices of Brighton & Hove.

"RIGHT," Mr Greenwood hollered. "Are we all ready?"

There were shouts of confirmation.

"Shiny!" Mr Greenwood exclaimed. "Frances, do you want to do the honours?"

Frances grinned, climbed onto the stone bench behind them, cupped her hands around her mouth, and then shouted: "WE ARE OPEN FOR BUSINESS!"

That announcement was met by cheers, and then the homeless people queued, most of them chattering. They took paper plates and held them out. Mr Greenwood served pieces of chicken, Tamara scooped pasta from a big pot, and Big John was filling bowls with soup.

Before long the queue began to shuffle past Amy and Frances, and the girls were kept busy handing out slices of bread and sprinkling cheese onto the pasta. Almost all of the people seemed to know Frances, and they greeted her fondly.

Little John came round, carrying two plates in his huge hands, both of them piled with food.

"Good food," he told Amy as she sprinkled liberal amounts of shredded cheese on the mountains of pasta on his plates.

Amy was pleased to see Hailey and Gaz in the queue, the both of them looking far more cheerful than they had been in front of St Bart's.

"Nice hat," Hailey said. "Looks good on you."

"Thanks!" Amy smiled, after which she turned to Gaz. "Have you seen the books?" She pointed behind her at the box filled with various paperbacks on one of the upper level tables.

"That I have," Gaz said. He stopped speaking to cough, before he continued, "my first point of call after I've eaten, thank you."

Some of the people passing by frightened Amy a little, not because they were threatening, but because they marked their presence loudly, shouting up and down the queue. She could tell though, that they weren't upset, just happy in their own way.

Other people passing by seemed much sadder, but their gratitude was real when they mumbled a 'thank you' after being served.

One was a very old lady, with a bent back, and tangled grey hair. Her hands were shaking and she asked Frances to butter her bread, after which she turned to Amy, pointing at one of the containers with biscuits.

"Could I have some biscuits?" She asked in a trembling voice.

"Of course," Amy answered, and worked the lid off the container. To her great surprise, the woman grabbed a whole handful of biscuits, and stuffed them in her coat pocket, after which she took another handful which also went into the pocket.

Amy frowned; it didn't seem very considerate towards the others, who might appreciate a biscuit as well. She glanced at Frances, who gave her a subtle shake of the head.

The queue began to thin, mostly consisting of people coming around for second helpings, including Little John whose appetite stretched to two full plates of seconds. With less to do, the cold became more noticeable, and they began to shiver a little.

One of the women at the coffee table next to them noticed. She had been serving cups of tea and coffee almost non-stop, greeting all comers with a friendly smile and a chat.

"How about a cup of tea?" She asked the girls.

"Thanks Clare!" Frances said.

"Milk and sugar?"

The girls both nodded. Amy noticed that the woman was wearing a small badge with Wilf's portrait on it, and the text 'Fiveways Wilf'.

Amy pointed at it. "I met Wilf just the other day."

"Isn't he adorable?" Clare asked. "I just love that cat." She handed both Amy and Frances a cup of steaming tea. "Speaking of cats, Frances, I'll drop by The Office this week to check on General, if that's alright."

"Thanks," Frances said. "I'll tell Dad."

The girls clutched their cold hands around the steaming cups.

"Does General live at The Office?" Amy asked Frances, recalling the tomcat's scarred face.

Frances took a sip of her tea. "Yep, just showed up one day, about two years ago. Walked in like he owned the place, no microchip or anything. Dad reckons it's handy having a cat prowling round The Office, he says it scares the mice. We feed General every day and he knows to use a litter tray. Clare takes him to the vets every now and then for shots and stuff."

"That lady, who took all of the biscuits," Amy said. "Is she homeless too?"

"No," Frances answered. "Some of the people here have a place to live, but they can't afford much food. Mrs Harwood has had her electricity cut off, because she couldn't pay her bills. Those biscuits are probably all she'll have to eat tonight."

"Oh! That's terrible! And the other really old people?"

Amy had seen a few grey-haired and white-bearded elderly men shuffle past, unsteady on their feet, their hands shaking.

"Most of those are homeless," Frances said.

Tamara joined them, flashing them a quirky smile before lighting a roll-up. "Mr O'Brian, that man with the cap on, he's got cancer, and most of the time he can't really think clearly anymore, that's why he lost his flat. They shut down his bank branch, and he was supposed to arrange all his payments online, but he really doesn't have a clue about computers."

"Is he dying?" Amy asked, recalling Gran's gaunt, almost skeletal face towards the end. "But surely..."

"They said he made himself intentionally homeless." Tamara shrugged. "So he's not getting any help. Welcome to twenty-first century Britain, Luv."

Amy repeated one of the expletives she'd heard Mr Greenwood use.

Tamara grinned. "I'm sure you're not supposed to be using that language."

"You're not supposed to smoke." Frances told her. "It's bad for your health."

Tamara looked at her roll-up with surprise. "Is it really? Never heard that one before."

"Mum and Dad think most homeless people are drug addicts," Amy said. "They say people have themselves to thank for being out on the street."

"A lot of people think that," Tamara answered. "There are a few, some of them here right now. They're still hungry, and thirsty. So we're not going to point at this one, or that one, and tell them they can't have a cup of soup. But most of the ones I know that use, didn't end up on the street because of that. Once on the street…," Tamara shrugged, "…The nights are long, cold, and full of fear. I personally don't blame them if they try to lose themselves for a few hours by having a drink, to be honest. I would."

Amy was startled by that admission, also because very few adults she knew would talk to a child like this, even if the child was nearly twelve years old. She liked the honesty of it. It also struck her that when Frances, Mr Greenwood or Tamara talked about homeless people, they didn't say things because they had read it in a newspaper somewhere. They said things because they actually knew the people on the streets, and had taken the time to listen to their stories.

Amy asked: "So most people here are not homeless because they were addicted?"

Tamara shook her head. "Nope. Big John used to be in the army, they sent him to Iraq and he came back wounded and all messed up in the head, so he ended up on the street. Gaz was an accountant for a big firm in London, but then he lost his job, became depressed and couldn't pay his rent anymore. Little John used to live in sheltered accommodation, but they closed that down, and then said he was well enough to take care of himself...well...have you talked to him at all?"

"Yes, I have," Amy answered.

"He's incredibly nice, wouldn't hurt a fly, but not very bright," Tamara said. "We take turns keeping an eye out on him."

"Like Big John the other day," Frances added.

Amy looked at Hailey, who was sitting on the bottom ledge of the Clock Tower, taking small bites from her plate. Gaz was sitting next to her, very protectively. Amy was concerned to hear him cough again. "And Hailey? Is Gaz her boyfriend?"

"No he's not," Tamara said. "She doesn't have a boyfriend, but Gaz looks after Hailey, especially at night, he kind of protects her. It's dangerous enough out on the streets. A lot of drunk people coming out of the pubs shout at rough sleepers, sometimes they even hit and kick them."

"Or pee on their sleeping bags," Frances said.

"No!" Amy could barely believe that people would do such things.

"Happens all the time, Luv," Tamara said. "People think it's okay to treat homeless people really badly. They've even doused sleeping bags with lighter fluid and set fire to them. And it's even more dangerous for women...you know..."

Though much about what happened between women and men was only vaguely understood by Amy, she knew enough to understand why it would be dangerous for women to be sleeping out on the streets. She shivered. "I thought bullies only really existed at school."

"I wish!" Frances said. "But adults are worse!"

A newcomer caught Amy's eye, a woman who looked totally out of place as she stepped up to Mr Greenwood. She had greying hair tied in bun and a remarkable face because her eyes sparkled with laughter and it was a sheer pleasure to behold her smile. She was dressed entirely in green men's clothes: a green shirt with old-fashioned cuff-links and a high collar, a suit of velvet dark green, offset by bright, almost luminous light green boots, and a shiny silk green neck-tie. She carried a basket and a twisted knobbly walking stick.

To Amy, the woman looked as if she had just stepped out of the Wyrde Woods from the *Secrets of the Wyrde Woods* series Amy loved reading. Her appearance formed a sharp contrast to Mr Greenwood, who was dressed in combat trousers and a battered old parka coat. Mr Greenwood appeared genuinely pleased to see the newcomer and shook her hand enthusiastically.

"That's Miss Puck," Frances told Amy. "She's got a shop in North Laine and supports Dad. I'm going to help Mrs Harwood select some things she might need, will you be alright?"

Amy nodded. Now that even Little John had eaten enough to satisfy his appetite, there was little for her to do but look around, and there was so much to see! She strolled over to the Clock Tower and sat down next to Hailey, for Gaz had left his place on the ledge to browse through the paperbacks. Many others were looking through the boxes as well.

Someone had brought a guitar, and started playing on it, strumming it randomly at first, before playing the opening chords of a song. People began to sing along. There were a group of youngish people wearing t-shirts with "Street Vets" printed on them, and they were visited by the rough sleepers who had brought along their dogs.

Hailey was deep in conversation with Tamara, about some mysterious thing they called 'Swep', so Amy decided to amuse herself. She opened her satchel and took out a sketching pad and pencil, and deftly started to capture the busy scene around the Clock Tower.

She had been at it for a while, when suddenly a woman's melodious voice exclaimed: "By Gemeeny, that looks fabulous!"

Amy looked up to see Miss Puck standing in front of her, staring at Amy's sketching pad with astonishment on her face.

"I'm sorry to disturb you," she quickly apologized. "But I was struck by your sketch…may I?"

Amy nodded and held out the pad. Miss Puck took it reverently, and began to examine it with a great deal of interest.

"I just love the angle you chose for this." She spoke enthusiastically. "The whole bird's eye point of view, looking down at the scene from the Clock Tower like a…"

"…Seagull," Amy said.

"Or an owl," Miss Puck said. "It reminds me of Gifman's work, but I don't suppose…"

"Jen Gifman!" Amy exclaimed. "Yes, I was thinking of her drawing of the encounter in Willikin's Drove in the…"

"…illustrated version of *Forgotten Road*!" Miss Puck cried out.

They beamed at each other.

"Always a pleasure to meet another fan," Miss Puck said. "My name is Miss Puck."

Amy already knew that, but decided not to point this out. "I'm Amy," she said instead. "A friend of Frances's."

"Frances Greenwood!" Miss Puck smiled. "A remarkable young lady, setting an example for us all."

Amy nodded.

"And extraordinarily fond of chocolate owls," Miss Puck added, mystifying Amy somewhat.

She retrieved a round business card from a pocket of her green coat and gave it to Amy. "Ask her to bring you to my shop sometime; I think you might like it."

Amy took the card, the front of which depicted a scroll with the words *The Owlery* written on them, above which vines of ivy curled around the image of a barn owl.

"Thallie," Miss Puck said, pointing at the owl.

"Joy Whitfield's owl!" Amy exclaimed. "What...?"

She was interrupted by Hailey, who suddenly hissed. "Get away from her!"

Amy looked at her, startled, because she thought Hailey was addressing Miss Puck, but Hailey wasn't looking at the green woman. Instead, she was staring intently at a portly man in a beige raincoat, who was talking to one of the young homeless women at the fringe of the busy scene around the Clock Tower, and handing her a small flier.

"Tom!" Hailey called out. "TOM!"

Mr Greenwood looked up from the pan he was scrubbing. Hailey pointed at the man in the raincoat, and Amy watched as a remarkable transformation came over Mr Greenwood's usually friendly face. His eyes hardened, his mouth became a grim line, and his nostrils flared up. He dropped the pan and took a step forward, shouting: "YOU!" at the man in the raincoat.

The strange man looked in Mr Greenwood's direction, irritation written on his face.

"We don't want the likes of you here," Mr Greenwood shouted angrily. "Get the HELL out of here. NOW!"

"Oh dear!" Miss Puck said nervously. Amy understood why, because the sight of the amiable Mr Greenwood consumed by fury was frightening to behold.

"Now, now, Tom," the man in the raincoat spoke in a tone which suggested Mr Greenwood was being entirely unreasonable. "It's a public space. I've as much right to be here as you have."

"GET THE HELL OUT OF HERE!" Mr Greenwood's hands curled into fists.

Big John stepped up next to Mr Greenwood, and put a hand on Mr Greenwood's arm, cautioning him. Gaz came to stand next to them as well, as did Frances.

The man in the raincoat shook his head. "You must stop pretending that you are the only one helping these poor people out, Tom. All I was doing was offering this young lady..," He indicated the homeless woman next to him, "...a roof over her head, a place to live. Surely that is no crime."

Mr Greenwood made to step forward, but he was restrained by Big John and Gaz.

Gaz looked at the man in the raincoat. "You had better go. Now."

The man shrugged, and then started backing off, before turning and walking away in the direction of Western Road.

Amy looked at Hailey, bewildered by the whole scene. "But if he was offering her..." she began to say.

Hailey was watching the man walk away, her face drawn in that hard mask of hers, but her voice was soft when she answered. "Martin Stoneleigh only ever offers young women one of his flats."

"Young women?" Miss Puck asked, sounding just as puzzled as Amy felt.

Hailey nodded, then looked Amy in the eyes. "He doesn't charge them rent, but he asks them for things he has no business asking for."

Amy's eyes widened. "You mean...sex?"

Hailey nodded grimly.

"Good grief!" Miss Puck exclaimed. "That's just sordid!"

"That is why Tom was so angry just now, Amy," Hailey said. "I hope you understand."

"I do," Amy replied. She was overwhelmed by a sense of great injustice, just as she had been when Frances and Tamara had told her people shouted at rough sleepers, and even peed on them as they were trying to sleep. This seemed even worse than that. Frances was right, adults could be far worse bullies than even the nastiest kids at school.

"It's a good thing," Miss Puck said slowly, "That Tom is here to keep an eye on things."

"Yes," Hailey said. "I don't know where we'd be without him."

The initially hushed murmurs after the confrontation between Mr Greenwood and the man in the raincoat were swelling to a greater volume again, although the general air of cheerfulness, which had marked the day so far, was replaced by a more sober mood.

When Amy helped clear up the tables shortly after, there was much to think about. The Sunday afternoon at the Clock Tower had provided a bewildering number of extreme opposites. On the one hand, there had been the sheer pleasure and beauty of people doing their best to help each other out, to provide some brightness in dark times. On the other hand, many of the things Frances had told Amy were heart-breaking or disturbing, some of it even plain evil. Humans, Amy decided, were capable of acts of tremendous kindness, but also of vile and selfish behaviour which she simply couldn't understand.

All in all though, Amy was glad she had come along to the Street Kitchen. Life had certainly become a whole lot more interesting since she had met Frances, Hailey, and Mr Greenwood, and she wondered briefly what further surprises lay in store for her.

END OF PART ONE

PART TWO

11. Walkabout in North Laine

Having a few hours to kill after school, Amy and Frances decided to visit North Laine. It was Amy's favourite destination in Brighton. The grid of streets between the station and Grand Parade was a curious mix of quiet residential streets and shopping streets, as well as many twittens, the whole area characterised by rows of cosy terraced cottages. The mainstay high street shops, which you could find in any town or city in the country, were restricted to the edges of North Laine. The heart of the neighbourhood consisted of small independent shops, quirky eating places, and generally anything weird and wonderful.

It was normally busy with out-of-town sightseers, students, and native Brightonians, all drawn to the vibrant colours, noisy pubs, and general bazaar-like atmosphere. It was less crowded this afternoon. Winter had made its presence known over recent days. Temperatures had plummeted, and a freezing wind seemed to blow straight through even the warmest winter coat.

Amy and Frances sought temporary reprieve from the cold in Snooper's Paradise, content to wander through the maze of bric-a-brac on display there. When they departed, they turned left to follow Kensington Gardens to Gloucester Road, intending to peek through the windows of the Ju-Ju clothes shop, as well as marvelling at the shop's colourful zebra-themed façade.

As always, Amy paused to admire the mosaic seagulls which decorated parts of the pavement on this bit of Gloucester Road. As she did so, she spotted two men begging outside of the newsagent opposite the Loot shop.

"Do you know those two?" Amy asked Frances.

"Yes," Frances answered curtly.

Amy was surprised at her tone. She was even more surprised when Frances took her hand and pulled Amy along with some haste, practically dragging her around the corner onto Sydney Street. She stopped in front of the Zoingimage copyshop.

"They know me too," Frances said, as if that clarified the matter.

"I don't understand."

"They're profs."

"Profs?" For a confusing moment Amy thought of university professors, but that didn't make sense.

"Professional beggars," Frances explained. "They've got a place to live, and get benefits, but they make extra money begging. To pay for their drink and drugs."

"Oh! That's what Mum said happens all the time."

"There aren't that many of them, but enough for people to say you can't trust rough sleepers asking for some change." Frances sounded disgusted.

"And they don't like you?" Amy asked, thinking of the haste with which Frances had pulled her away.

"Not so much me as Dad. He's told them off before and they don't like that."

"Ha! Serves them right."

Amy began to laugh, but her laugh died down when she saw the expression on Frances's face.

"It's serious, Amy. The profs can get abusive. Violent. They threatened to beat Dad up."

Amy felt bad about laughing. "Seriously? They threatened your dad? What did he do?"

"Rolled up his shirt sleeves and invited them to have a go." Frances shook her head. "They backed off, but I don't think it was very clever of him."

"I suppose you have to be careful with people on the street."

"Deffo. And not just the profs. Even the ones you know from the Street Kitchen."

"How come?"

"Sometimes they'll have a drink, or something else. To forget where they are for a few hours."

"Even Hailey and Gaz, people like that?"

"Even them." Frances confirmed. "If you see them around, don't walk straight up to them. Like, check if they are behaving strangely first."

"Strange? How do I know?"

"You'll know."

"But..."

"They'll talk weird, like real slow, or bloody fast. Move funny too, as if they could fall over any moment. Or frozen like a statue, just staring at nothing."

"Oh." Amy's disappointment must have shown on her face, for all of a sudden Frances laughed, and gave her a playful shove.

"Just be careful, that's all. It doesn't happen often, not our lot anyway. And if you don't know them, just stay away."

Amy nodded, somewhat crestfallen. "I was hoping that...you know...there'd be a difference between good and bad..."

Frances nodded. "I know what you mean." She took out her phone and glanced at the time. "We should go for the bus. Catch it at St Peter's?"

They walked on down Sydney Street, past the Bonsai shop, Curiouser & Curiouser and the Great Frog jewellery shop, Brighton Guitars and Dave's Comics. They took a right turn to head down Gloucester Street, past Bomb hairdresser's, where they duly giggled at the Star Wars toys arranged in an obscene display.

Frances was asking loads of questions about Jacob, fascinated by the idea of having a baby brother.

"Do you dress him up?"

"Er, no."

"You should, maybe you can bring him to The Office, and we'll take him into Aladdin's Cave."

Amy laughed. "Mum would have a right fit if I tried that. Your dad was brill, by the way, when I called him about the Street Kitchen. I was afraid he was going to tell them too much."

"We were lucky," Frances said. "He thought they knew."

"He thought what?!"

"He probably wouldn't have taken you, if he knew your parents were dead set against it." Frances shrugged. "I didn't tell him everything now, did I?"

Amy's mouth dropped open. "But..."

"Shoot!" Frances grabbed Amy's arm. "The Trolls!"

Amy looked ahead, along Gloucester Street. They were nearing the busy intersection where Richmond Place, Gloucester Place, and St George's Place met, close to St Peter's Church. The three Year 9 girls had just turned the corner, by the North Laine Brewhouse, in the company of two older boys, with cropped hair and dressed in track suits. The five were talking, or rather shouting all at once, making a noisy procession up Gloucester Street.

"Quick!" Amy pulled Frances into St George's Mews, the narrow street to their right.

They started walking down it fast.

"Do you think they saw us?" Frances asked.

"I don't know," Amy said. Her throat was dry, and her heart beating faster.

"OI! YOU!" They heard a Troll shout behind them.

"It's Freckle Face and Snowflake!" Another Troll hollered.

"RUN!" Amy and Frances said simultaneously, and started legging it down St George's Mews.

"CATCH THEM!" One of the Trolls yelled, and the girls could hear the pounding of feet behind them.

"We gotta…stop…meeting…like this…" Frances panted.

Amy couldn't help but laugh, although it sounded more like a panicked gasp than anything else.

When they reached the end of St George's Mews, with the Trolls beginning to gain on them, Amy made to go right, towards the St Peter's bus stops. It was usually busy there, and there might be safety in having lots of people around.

"No!" Frances shook her head, and pulled Amy the other way. "Pelham Square."

Pelham Square wasn't far. At its centre was a small, fenced park. The girls burst through the gate, into the grassy centre of the park which seemed empty. The Trolls slowed down after they came through the gate. Amy and Frances ran to the centre of the park, and then turned to face their pursuers.

"That was stupid," one of the Trolls said. "We got you now!"

Amy was frightened, but also surprised to hear Frances mutter very softly: "Oh no, you don't."

"STOOOPID!" Another Troll hollered.

"They're just little girls." One of the boys frowned.

"They disrespected us," the third Troll told him. "Dissed us and disrespected us."

Frances smiled. Amy, her heart pounding, didn't understand why.

"They need to be taught some manners," the first Troll grinned evilly.

"Snowflake and Freckle Face," the second Troll pronounced with satisfaction. "Are mates with smelly tramps and bums, aintcha, you little Ginger Freak?"

"WHO YOU CALLING GINGER FREAK?"

The voice was so loud that it seemed to fill all of Pelham Square; female, and filled with raging fury. Amy spun around. There was a corner of grass, concealed behind some bushes which she hadn't noticed before. There were bags there, and that curious mishmash of homeless bedding. People getting up, one rising to his feet, the other striding towards the centre of the park.

"YOU CALLING ME A GINGER FREAK?!"

It was Hailey.

Amy had seen Hailey's hard expression before, but that faded next to the feral, angry snarl Hailey showed now, her eyes spitting fire.

"And who are you calling tramps?" Big John joined Hailey.

He spoke very softly, yet there was an ominous menace in his calmness.

Amy turned to look at the Trolls and their boys. All five looked frightened, dead scared.

"They said *'smelly'* tramps," Frances shouted, unable to keep the delight out of her voice. She nudged Amy, who could still barely believe how fast the tables had turned.

"Frances! Amy!" Little John lumbered to stand next to Big John and Hailey. He grinned at them happily, then looked at the Trolls and the boys with a question on his face. "These are your friends?" He lumbered forwards, hands outstretched. "Hello, I am…"

One of the Trolls screamed, another backed up but tripped over her own feet, falling hard on the grass.

"I'll call the police!" The third Troll shrieked, her voice conveying nothing but shrill panic.

"Go on. We ain't done nothing," Hailey barked.

"Yet…" Big John added meaningfully.

"Listen mate, we don't want no trouble," one of the boys said nervously.

"No trouble!" Little John ambled forward, hands outstretched with his palms outwards.

His slow advance was the final straw for the boys, who made towards the gate. The Troll who had fallen scrambled up, and the three Year 9 girls stumbled towards the gate as well, in blind panic.

Amy felt satisfaction seeing them like this.

Now they know what it's like, to be scared.

It wasn't until they were back on the street, with some distance between them and the people in the park, that the Trolls hollered some choice insults, before making themselves scarce.

Hailey's face relaxed. Big John grinned. Little John looked confused.

The girls joined them.

"They're gonna kill us now," Amy predicted, but she was smiling.

"Oh!" Frances laughed. "Deffo, but it was worth it, every second of it. Did you see them freak out?"

"I'm sorry I scared your friends." Little John looked glum.

"No!" Frances shook her head. "You were brill, Little John, absolutely cracking."

"I was?" Little John looked surprised.

"You did well, Little John," Hailey assured him, then cast a glance at Amy. "You okay, Luv?"

Amy nodded, and turned to Frances. "You knew?!"

"There's usually somebody here," Frances said. "And I saw them before we ran into the park, I knew where to look."

"You know those misfits?" Big John enquired.

"From school," Amy said. "They bully all the Year Sevens."

"I hate bullies," Hailey spat on the ground. "That was fun, but we're not gonna be around all the time."

Frances nodded grimly. "We'll have to be clever."

"Well, if there's anybody who can outsmart them, it'll be you," Big John ruffled Frances's hair and she smiled at him.

"We were on our way to the bus stop," Amy said. "But..."

"I don't think they'll lie in wait," Big John assured her. "But we'll walk you to the bus, just to be sure."

Amy smiled gratefully.

The three homeless people gathered their belonging, then they all left the park, heading towards St Peter's.

"Where is Gaz?" Amy asked Hailey.

Hailey looked sad. "He's gone to the doctor's, the homeless doctor at Morley Street."

"What's wrong with him?" Amy recalled Gaz's recurring cough at the Street Kitchen. "Is it that cough?"

Hailey nodded. "It's worse, he's got it bad."

"Dr Worthley will patch him up. He always helps us out." Big John said. He addressed Frances. "You on the way to The Office?"

She nodded.

"Rather you than me," Big John said. "Your dad's in a foul mood."

"Tell me about it." Frances sighed.

"Why?" Amy asked.

"SWEP," Hailey answered.

"Swep?" Amy recalled hearing the word before, but she had no idea what it meant.

"Severe Weather Emergency Protocol," Big John told her.

"When it's this cold," Frances added. "They're meant to open an emergency night shelter. So rough sleepers have a dry and warm place to sleep."

"But they haven't yet," Hailey said, a dark cloud on her face. "They say it's gotta to freeze for three nights before they do."

"So you're meant to stay out for three nights?" Amy asked, suddenly acutely aware how cold it felt, and had been feeling for days now. "It's freezing!"

Big John shrugged. "Here in Brighton, they don't take the wind factor into account, and they measure the temperature in the warmest part of town."

"WHY?" Amy was appalled.

"It saves them money and trouble, I suppose." Hailey said.

"Dad's furious," Frances told Amy. "He's been calling and emailing the Council, but they're ignoring him."

"Business as usual." Big John shrugged. "We'll make do, but for those who are poorly, like Gaz, it can make a big difference."

"People could die!" Amy exclaimed.

"People do, Luv," Hailey said.

"Dr Worthley said fifty people died last year, all related to homelessness," Big John added.

"FIFTY?!"

Big John nodded. "Fifty deaths, I suppose it's one way of solving the homeless crisis."

Amy was shocked, and couldn't understand why the others laughed at Big John's last comment.

"And you know what happens when a homeless person dies and gets to Heaven's gates, right?" Hailey asked.

Amy shook her head. Frances grinned. Big John snorted.

"They're sent away," Hailey said. "Because..."

"They haven't got a local connection," Big John completed.

There was renewed laughter at that, Little John adding his booming guffaws this time.

Amy shook her head in disbelief. She didn't think that was funny at all, but on second thought, she decided that the others probably didn't think so either, not really anyway.

Maybe, sometimes all you can do with so much bad luck, is to just laugh at it.

11.5. Crisis on North Street

A few days later Amy was walking down North Street towards Old Steine to catch a bus home. She had been in the Jubilee Library to look up information for a history essay, after which she'd gone to a shop in town to peek at the illustrated *Secrets of the Wyrde Woods* books.

It was yet another cold day, made worse by the icy wind. It was bearable when Amy was moving, but she hoped she wouldn't have to wait for the bus too long. There were less people on North Street than usual, and none were lingering by the many shop windows. Instead, almost everybody moved with an urgency that betrayed their wish to be out of the cold as soon as possible. Even the busy traffic seemed to move with increased speed, bus after bus rushing by, filled to the brim with passengers heading home after a day at school or work.

At first, Amy didn't pay much attention to the commotion on the pavement ahead of her. It was a rare day in Brighton on which something odd didn't happen. One day she might expect to spot the Disco Bunny, or one of the many other local eccentric characters. On the next day, she'd have to take a detour around the antics of stag and hen parties. There were usually buskers around, or other performers. Then there were those days when the whole city gathered in a collective madness, dressed up or not for the occasion, and sometimes not dressed at all.

Her first inkling that something was wrong was gleaned from muttered comments by people coming from the opposite direction.

"...disgraceful..."

"...Mum, that man scared me!"

"...don't mind what they use to take their mind off things...but must it be in plain sight?"

"...shouldn't be allowed..."

"...getting worse and worse..."

"...no shame at all..."

Amy looked ahead. Something was going on in front of the North Street Co-Op. People were speeding up as they walked past, and giving a wide berth to the space immediately in front of the Co-Op window. She could also hear strange sounds, even over the rush of traffic. It was an odd contrast between a monotonous mewling and hoarse barking, like some animal in distress.

Curious, Amy slowed down as she approached.

"...this country is going down the drain..."

"...someone should call the police..."

"...pleazhelpus...pleazpleazpleaz...pleazhelpus..."

"...should be locked up..."

"...pleazpleazpleaz...pleazhelpus...pleazhelpus..."

There was a pile of bedding in front of the Co-Op, someone curled up in a sleeping bag, shaking.

Little John was in front of the bedding, on his knees, his huge arms stretched in front of him, and his large gnarled hands opened to the passing people in supplication. He looked distraught. Large tears were rolling down his cheeks.

"...pleazpleazpleaz...pleazhelpus...pleaz...PLEAZ!"

He howled the last word at the top of his voice, startling some of the passer-bys.

Remembering what Frances had told her about being careful, Amy approached Little John slowly, staying out of his reach when she called out to him.

"Little John."

"...pleazpleaz..." Little John was shaking his head to and fro.

"Little John!"

This time he looked up and around him, hope and fear mixed on his tear-stained face. His eyes found Amy.

"Pleaz...Amy...I'm scared...I'm scared...pleazhelpus..."

"Hey you, girl," a voice sounded behind her. "Stay away from him."

Amy ignored the voice, maintaining eye contact with Little John. She forced a smile.

Gotta keep smiling. Someone's gotta smile.

"It's going to be alright, Little John," Amy said.

Little John shook his head in wild denial. "No...no...no..."

"It will be alright." Amy insisted with a confidence she didn't feel. "What happened, Little John? What's the matter?"

"Gaz," Little John indicated the pile of bedding behind him. "Gaz is sick. Gaz is sick. I'm scared, Amy!"

Suddenly, the curled form of the sleeping bag straightened like an unleashed spring, and then shook violently as the occupant was caught up in a series of racking coughs.

Throwing all caution to the wind, Amy rushed to Gaz's side. "Gaz! Gaz?"

The coughing stopped, and Gaz gulped at the air, his lungs wheezing.

"Gaz?" Amy laid a hand on his shoulder.

Gaz responded to her voice, or the touch of her hand, by shifting his head sideways in her direction. There was no recognition in his eyes. They rolled sightlessly in their sockets as Gaz was racked by another series of savage upheavals of his lungs.

With shock, Amy registered that his face was turning blue.

She turned towards the passer-bys on the street. Little John looked at her hopefully, until she started calling for help.

"Help us please! I need help!" Amy shouted.

"...pleazhelpus...pleazhelpus..." Little John restarted his litany.

"HELP! I need help!"

To Amy's utter horror, nobody stopped.

Nobody at all.

There were plenty of adults passing by, but all hastened their step. Most avoided looking at her. Those she managed to get eye contact with, looked swiftly away, their faces hard, or twitching with embarrassment.

"...pleazhelpus...pleazpleazpleaz..."

Frances! What do I do?

Frances wasn't here though. Amy was. She called out for help one more time, in a last effort to enlist some support, any support, but it was to no avail. She, Gaz and Little John might as well have been invisible.

Amy grabbed her phone and dialled 999.

"999 emergency, which service do you..."

"I need an ambulance!" Amy shouted. "It's Gaz, he can hardly breathe! He's turning blue!"

"My God, this town is becoming the pits."

"What is your location please?"

Gaz dissolved into another bout of barking coughs, wheezing as he tried to draw in breath between the coughs.

"Shameful!"

"...pleazhelpus...pleazhelpus..."

"I'm on North Street, in Brighton, in front of the Co-Op."

"North Street Co-Op. One second..."

"Lazy, good-for-nothing, work-shy junkies."

"...Right, what is your name?"

"My name is Amy. Amy Wheatley. Please, tell them to hurry, I think he's choking!

"...pleazhelpuspleazhelpuspleazhelpus..."

"Bloody drunks!"

SHUT UP! Just shut up!

"Ambulance is on the way, Amy." The operator said. "Is your dad conscious, is he responding to you?"

There was no time to rectify the 'dad'.

"...pleazpleazpleazpleazpleaz...helpus..."

"No! His eyes are rolling, I don't think he recognises me. He's choking."

"They should round them all up...send them to special camps on the Downs or something."

"Listen carefully, Amy, here's what I want you to do. Take a deep breath, okay, and then sit with your dad, and talk to him, just keep on talking to him until the ambulance shows up."

"Yes, okay, I'll do that. Please hurry," Amy put her phone in her pocket.

Little John looked at her, desperation on his face. "Helpus?"

"Yes, Little John, help is on the way." Amy crouched by Gaz's side. He let out one last hoarse cough, and then shuddered all over. One of his arms was lolling out of the sleeping bag, and Amy took his hand into her own.

"It'll be alright, Gaz, I called an ambulance," Amy told Gaz, who let out a groan.

Amy turned to Little John, who was staring blankly at passerbys, this time without any pleas for help on his lips, although he was sobbing loudly. "Little John, come sit next to me. Come here."

"Come there?" Little John asked.

"Yes, we need to talk to Gaz, do you understand, we need to talk to him."

Little John crawled over to Amy's side. "I can talk."

"I know you can, Little John," Amy said. "Tell Gaz what you had for breakfast."

Little John's face lit up. "Bacon! I had bacon for breakfast."

"Did you hear that, Gaz? Little John had bacon for breakfast."

What followed was the most absurd conversation Amy had ever had, barring the times when Jacob babbled nonsensical words at her. She held on to Gaz's hand tightly, and kept Little John chatting away about his breakfast and lunch. The tears on the big man's face dried up, and he seemed to have forgotten all about Gaz's predicament as he talked food.

Gaz had another coughing fit, shaking violently again, heaving for air. Little John looked as alarmed as Amy felt, but she made herself smile at him. "Gaz'll be okay, Little John, it'll be alright."

"I'm scared." Little John said, when Gaz stopped coughing. He looked embarrassed, "I'm sorry I'm scared. I know I'm not supposed to be scared. I'm sorry."

"It's okay," Amy told him. "No need for Little John to be sorry, is there, Gaz?"

"No need?" Little John sounded suspicious.

"I'll tell you a secret, Little John. Can you keep a secret?"

The big man nodded earnestly.

"I am scared too," Amy said.

"You?" Little John's eyes grew wide. "Really?"

"Yes. Promise. Cross my heart and hope to die. It's okay to be scared."

It's okay to be scared.

Inwardly, Amy wasn't scared, she was terrified. She bit on her lip. It had been good, she felt, to tell Little John because it seemed to make him feel better, but she instinctively knew that she shouldn't show him that fear. If she stayed calm, he was more likely to stay calm too. It was dreadful how upset Little John was, as inconsolable as Jacob could be sometimes, but Little John was much older than Jacob and that made her feel terribly sad.

Gaz shot upright, his free hand clutching at his chest as he tried to wheeze a breath in. He failed to inhale much air, because the process was interrupted by renewed coughing.

"That sounds worse. Has it become worse?" A Co-Op staff member came walking out of the shop, a man whose face showed genuine concern. He took one look at Gaz's face, and reached for a trouser pocket. "I'm calling an ambulance."

"I've called already," Amy said. "They're on their way."

Please stay, please stay.

"Oh well done!" The Co-Op man came closer. "Did they say how long they'd be?"

Just then, they could hear the banshee wails of an ambulance, approaching rapidly from the direction of Old Steine.

"Oh good," the Co-Op man said. "Sometimes it can take so long these days."

"Are you alright?" he asked Amy.

Amy wasn't really, dazed by all that was happening, but she nodded anyway.

Gaz coughed, but only a single time.

"Hang on in there, Gaz," the Co-Op man told him, then looked at Little John. "You okay there, John?"

Little John didn't pay him attention, engrossed as he was by the approaching yellow and green van, its siren screaming and lights flashing.

During the wait for the ambulance, every second had seemed to last for an hour. Upon its arrival, time seemed to speed up, everything became a blur. The ambulance crew were brisk, tending to Gaz even as they asked Amy and the Co-Op man a lot of questions. A stretcher was fetched, and Gaz transferred to it. They lifted him up. One of them looked at Amy.

"Come on, Luv. We'll take you and your dad to A&E at the Royal Sussex."

Amy began to shake her head, but then decided that she didn't want Gaz to be on his own. She looked at Little John. Could she leave him alone?

"Amy, I'm scared," the big man said, looking at Gaz on the stretcher with wide eyes.

The Co-Op man came to her rescue. "I bet you're hungry too, John."

He knows them! He used their names.

"Hungry?" Little John looked at the Co-Op man, puzzled for a moment, but then he began to nod with conviction "Food?" He asked hopefully.

The Co-Op man winked at Amy, then smiled at Little John. "Yes John, food, why don't you come inside with me, we'll see what we can find."

Little John rose to his feet. "Can I have a tuna sandwich? I like tuna."

"Of course you can!" The Co-Op man led Little John towards the shop entrance, turning his head long enough to give Amy a little nod. She nodded back briefly, and then ran towards the ambulance, to be helped into the back by one of the crew.

"Strap yourself in. Keep talking to him," the crew member said, before shutting the door.

Talking about what? Amy secured her seatbelt, and looked at Gaz, who looked dreadfully vulnerable on his stretcher.

"You all buckled up back there?" The driver called through the cab window.

"Yes!" Amy shouted back. The ambulance lurched into movement. Amy recalled that Gaz liked to read books, so she began to tell him about the books she had read, and kept that up until the ambulance reached the Royal Sussex County Hospital on Edward Street.

12. At the Sussex on Edward Street

Amy waited in a hospital corridor, fretting at the passage of time, which crept by oh so slowly. She tried calling Frances, but her friend didn't pick up her phone.

Amy felt alone, even more friendless than she had been in front of the Co-Op when everybody had just walked on by, pretending not to see Gaz's predicament, or Amy and Little John's despair. At least then, she'd had Little John for company.

Amy decided to send Frances a text message and opened a text screen on her phone. She stared at the blinking cursor blankly for a moment. How to start? 'Hey I'm in hospital' wouldn't be the best of openings. In the end she settled for:

>*Gaz is really ill. He's in hospital*<

That left Frances unaware of Amy's own whereabouts. Amy wasn't sure what Frances could do if she knew, but at least letting her friend know would satisfy the strong urge Amy felt to let somebody know where she was, and she could hardly call her parents.

>*I'm with him*<

That matter settled, Amy returned to fidgeting impatiently. She nearly jumped up every time people passed through the corridor. Two doctors, deep in discussion about some complicated procedure. Nurses carrying clipboards, pushing trolleys, or walking past with clean bedding in their arms. A million-year-old man, back hunched as he inched by, leaning on his walking frame. A boy Amy's age, pale and silent as he was pushed by in a wheelchair.

Finally, a nurse walked purposefully towards Amy. The nurse's bedraggled, brown hair was bundled in a sloppy pony tail, and she had deep shadows under her tired eyes. She was carrying a clipboard, and said: "I need to ask you some more questions, is that alright?"

Amy nodded. "Is Gaz going to be okay?"

"He'll pull through, he's in good hands now. Can you tell me where you and your dad live?"

"He's homeless, he lives on the street."

The nurse looked puzzled at that.

"He's not my father," Amy explained. "There was confusion...it was confusing...they thought he was, and I wanted to stay with him."

"What is your relation to him then? How do you know this man?"

The nurse sounded suspicious, and that unsettled Amy. Back on North Street, in front of the Co-Op, she had felt...Amy searched for the right word...responsible. She had felt responsible for Gaz. She hadn't asked for that responsibility. It had been cast upon her shoulders because nobody would help. Nobody.

Amy shuddered, as she recalled her near panic...Gaz choking...Little John's frightful upset. She had felt responsible for the big man too. He had been as helpless as a small child.

Getting into the ambulance with Gaz had been a logical thing to do, to see it through. Now Amy realised that it appeared odd, strange, out of the ordinary.

"Well?" The nurse asked, frowning now. She was beginning to scare Amy a little.

"He's a nice man," Amy blurted out. "He's clever, he likes reading books, he protects Hailey on the streets at night...I...

...I like him. He's a friend, not like Frances, but a friend like Hailey.

"Do your parents know you are here? That you were in town with this man?"

No, they'd kill me if they knew. The thought made Amy laugh nervously.

"Right, I think we'd better call your parents, don't you?"

Amy shook her head. Her lungs felt constricted. Her heart started to beat faster.

The nurse took a step forward, panicking Amy who darted to the right, and then ducked beneath the nurse's arm —which was reaching out for her— and legged it down the hospital corridor.

"WAIT!" The nurse shouted. "STOP! COME BACK!"

Amy ignored her, bursting through a set of swinging doors, dodging out of the way of two male nurses rolling an empty hospital bed along, weaving through a family carrying cards, flowers and a chocolates, and then —spotting daylight— rushing towards the exit.

She could hear commotion behind her, the nurse was in pursuit, shouting for hospital security.

Amy dashed through the outer door...

...straight into Frances and Mr Greenwood.

"Amy?!" Frances's eyes widened.

"Lass!" Mr Greenwood exclaimed. "What's the matter?"

Amy blinked with surprise, but when she registered that it really was Frances, she threw herself into her friend's arms with a loud sob, and held her tight.

"It's okay," Frances said softly. "It's going to be okay."

"Poor girl," Mr Greenwood ruffled Amy's hair. "You really have been in the wars, haven't you?"

Amy withdrew from Frances's embrace, not caring that tears were streaming down her face. "Nobody would help, Mr Greenwood, nobody even stopped!"

"There she is!" The nurse stepped outside, flanked by a security guard, and a doctor with a stethoscope dangling from her neck. "That's the girl, Dr Sengupta."

Frances stepped to Amy's side, and clutched Amy's hand, giving it a reassuring squeeze.

The doctor was of Indian descent, and had a kind, understanding face. She peered at Amy for a moment, and then looked at Mr Greenwood. "Tom!"

"Hullo, Padmaja," Mr Greenwood answered. He took a step forward, to stand at Amy's other side, and laid his hand on Amy's shoulder. His hand was warm and comforting. "The girl's with me."

Doctor Sengupta looked relieved. "Well, that'll do for me."

"But Doctor!" The nurse protested.

The doctor held up her hand. "If Tom Greenwood vouches for the girl, then there's nothing to worry about. Now I suggest we get inside, out of the cold."

They went back inside, Amy somewhat reluctantly. Mr Greenwood handed Frances a tenner, and told her to treat both herself and Amy to something to drink in the little coffee shop. Then he followed Doctor Sengupta down a corridor, the nurse trailing behind them.

Frances bought two hot chocolates and two brownies.

"Chocolate!" She declared. "Nothing beats chocolate in a crisis."

Amy smiled at that. It wasn't much of a smile, but she could feel herself relaxing, the tension of the afternoon ebbing away at last.

"How did you know I was here?" She asked, still trying to make sense of what seemed a miraculous appearance.

"Mr Mackellow called Dad," Frances explained.

"Mr who?"

"He works at the North Street Co-Op. He told Dad that they had taken Gaz to the Sussex, with a red-haired girl in school uniform, so we figured that was you."

Amy recalled that the Co-Op Man had known both Gaz and Little John by name. "Little John! Oh, Frances! He was so upset, but this Mr Mackellow calmed him down."

"Dad called Tamara, she's gone to the Co-Op to look after Little John. He'll be alright. Did he ask Mr Mackellow for a tuna sandwich?"

"Yes!"

"They're good people at the Co-Ops. Don't chase them away, like some other places do."

"I tried calling you!"

Frances looked crestfallen. "I went with Dad to make a delivery and left my phone at The Office."

Amy took a sip of her hot chocolate, relieved that things were falling into place. "How does your dad know that doctor?"

"Malnutrition."

"Huh? What?"

"It's when people don't have enough to eat…"

"I know that! I'm not that stupid, I just don't get what that has to do with your Dad."

"There's lots of malnutrition in the city. Old people. Poor people. The hospital call social services, but they take forever to do anything about it. So doctors, like Doctor Sengupta, also call Dad, and we make sure they have food."

"Oh, that's good."

"Not always." Frances grimaced. "Sometimes when social services finally visit, they see food in the cupboards and then say that people had been telling fibs. That'll have Dad hollering at them on the phone for sure. So, how bad was it at the Co-Op?"

"I felt so lonely," Amy said. "There were loads of people, Frances. I was calling for help. So was Little John. And they all just walked past."

"Bloody hell. Tell me everything."

Amy did, reliving it all as she spoke, but much more calmly this time. When she was finished, Mr Greenwood reappeared.

"Gaz is going to be okay," he told the girls. "It was touch and go for a bit, but he's sedated now, and sleeping."

Amy sighed with relief, Gaz was in good hands and a weight seemed to slip off her shoulders.

"There's not much we can do right now by staying here," Mr Greenwood added. "And it's getting late, so we'll give you a lift home, Amy."

13. Confession on Ditchling Road

"You can drop me off at the Fiveways shops," Amy suggested as they passed The Level park. It had got dark outside, and Amy was conscious that Mum would be home any minute now.

"Oh, I don't think so," Mr Greenwood answered. He steered the van onto Ditchling Road. "Not after what you've been through today. I'll take you home, and have a word with your parents."

Amy and Frances exchanged a worried glance.

"Amy will be fine," Frances suggested. "And we've got that food delivery for Mrs Mitchell, remember? All the way in Portslade..."

"I'll be okay, Mr Greenwood," Amy said, as earnestly as she could. "It's just a short walk home from the shops."

"That may be," Mr Greenwood answered cheerfully. "But I'm dropping you right on your front doorstep."

"Dad...!"

"Mr Greenwood...!"

Mr Greenwood cast a glance sideways at the girls, and his brow furrowed. "You two had better tell me what's going on then."

"Nothing," the girls answered in unison.

"I wasn't born yesterday." Mr Greenwood shook his head. "If it had been Frances today, at the Co-Op, I'd want to...never mind. I'm taking you home, Amy, and I want a word with your parents. Explain to them..."

"Dad, she'll get into trouble!" Frances blurted out.

"Trouble? Why?"

Amy closed her eyes in desperation, seeking some sort of escape.

"Frances," Mr Greenwood said. His voice was uncharacteristically strict. "You know how I feel about honesty."

"Dad, I..."

"She hasn't been telling fibs, Mr Greenwood," Amy said quickly. "My parents...they don't like homeless people, they told me to stay away from them. Frances is right, if you talk to them about today, I'll get into trouble."

"And you didn't think to tell me this before I took you to the Sunday Street Kitchen?" Mr Greenwood sounded incredulous.

"I really wanted to go!" Amy exclaimed.

"So they had no idea?"

"Just that...there was a catering job, Mr Greenwood." Amy suddenly felt ashamed. She had been telling herself that no real lies had been told, neither to her parents, nor to Mr Greenwood.

"Listen to me, Amy," Mr Greenwood said. "I like you, you're a brave girl, and Frances has found a good friend in you. But you've made me complicit in deceit, and that isn't something I can appreciate a great deal."

Amy nodded unhappily. "I'm sorry."

"But, Dad..."

"None of your nonsense, Frances," Mr Greenwood growled. "You may not have lied outright, but you've fooled me and I don't like it. Amy is welcome at The Office, and the Street Kitchen, but her parents need to know, and give permission."

Amy felt her chest go tight. She had so hoped to avoid this, tried to escape from the nurse at the Sussex even, to prevent a phone call to her parents. It was bad enough that Mr Greenwood sounded so disappointed, but she couldn't even begin to imagine how Mum would react. Amy recalled that tight grip on her arm, the fury in Mum's voice.

She sought Frances's hand, and clutched it hard.

Mr Greenwood noticed, and sighed. "It's not going to be the end of the world, girls. Nothing that a good chat won't sort out."

"Yes, Mr Greenwood," Amy said dully, but she didn't believe a word of it. He was kind, funny, and clever, but he didn't know Amy's parents. She stayed silent, trying to breathe slowly to counter the growing sense of dread she felt, her tummy a bottomless pit.

That dread became worse when they approached Amy's home. Her heart started beating loudly when Mr Greenwood parked the van, began pounding when they walked up the front garden path, and Amy thought she'd faint when Mr Greenwood rang the doorbell.

Dad opened, looking puzzled as he took in the delegation on his doorstep. "Amy?"

"Mr Wheatley," Mr Greenwood said. "I'm Tom Greenwood. We've spoken on the phone."

"So we have," Dad said, and then smiled at Frances. "And you must be Frances?"

Frances nodded.

"Nice to meet you," Dad said. He stretched out a hand to Mr Greenwood, who shook it.

"I hate to impose, Mr Wheatley," Mr Greenwood said. "But I'm afraid that we need to talk, about what these two rascals of ours have got up to."

Amy shut her eyes tightly and despaired, in the knowledge that all hell was about to break loose.

14. Facing the Music in Fiveways

The end of the world started with an absurd spell of the perfectly ordinary. Not entirely, perhaps, because it was somewhat strange for Amy to see Frances and Mr Greenwood in her living room. They seemed out of context somehow, but Amy supposed that was the newness of it. She had hoped that Frances would visit her home one day soon, but she hadn't imagined that it would be anything like this.

When Dad announced there were visitors, Mum rose to introduce herself to Mr Greenwood and Frances. She was all smiles, which just made Amy feel worse, because she doubted those smiles would last once Mr Greenwood told her parents why he wanted to talk to them. The storm which loomed over her caused Amy's belly to cramp into a fist-sized ball of cold, hard marble.

"You must be Jacob!" Frances's voice broke Amy away from her dark thoughts.

She looked to see Frances drop on her knees in front of Jacob, who stared at her with wide eyes, sucking his thumb.

"Aren't you a gorgeous little man!" Frances exclaimed. She looked at Amy, her elfin features animated by sheer delight. "Isn't he adorable?"

Amy had to admit that Jacob appeared a bundle of cuteness, the way he was staring shyly at Frances. There was no trace of the little tyke Amy's baby brother could also be, demanding attention, chewing on her pencils if Amy didn't keep an eagle eye on them, throwing his toys about in wild abandon, or screaming in a tantrum.

Amy's heart skipped a beat when she heard Mr Greenwood mention her name. Focusing on the adult conversation, Amy learned that there was to be a stay of execution, for the adults agreed that tea should be offered and accepted.

Dad and Mr Greenwood disappeared into the kitchen. Mum looked at Frances and Jacob, smiling approval.

"Do you get to baby-sit him!" Frances asked.

Amy nodded dumbly, thrown by Frances's formulation, which suggested it was a privilege to do so, like a high honour. Though Jacob had his moments, mostly Amy experienced looking after him like an obstacle that made it impossible to spend a quiet hour reading a book, or creating whole new worlds on a blank sheet of paper with nothing more than a few pencils as tools.

"Lucky you!" Frances looked genuinely envious.

Amy shook her head, trying to search for words to explain that it only took a blink of an eye for Jacob to turn from an adorable cutie-pie to a terrible monster that had crawled out of Hove Lagoon. Failing to find the right words, and aware that Mum was listening in on them, Amy said instead: "On the weekends mostly, especially Saturday afternoons."

"I'm sure, Frances," Mum said, "That Amy would love to have you over to help her baby-sit Jacob."

"Really? Thank you!" Frances clasped her hands. "Do you hear that, Jacob? We'll get to play."

Jacob solemnly handed Frances one of his brightly coloured building blocks, which Frances proceeded to examine with great interest. Mum encouraged him to find more, and Jacob began to stumble around on his short little legs, gathering them, making a pile in front of Frances.

Mum likes Frances now. She's being nice to her, but when she finds out...

Amy grimaced at the thought of Frances's hopes to baby-sit Jacob being dashed. It wasn't fair on her friend.

She felt dizzy with tension when all but Jacob gathered around the dinner table. They took a seat and mugs of steaming tea were distributed. Jacob had followed Frances like a puppy, and seemed happy to lean against her leg, gazing up at the frequent smiles Frances directed at him.

"We need to talk some…" Mr Greenwood announced. He looked at Frances, then at Amy. "The girls haven't been entirely honest with us."

"Oh?" Mum's forehead showed the beginning of a frown.

Frances shrugged, before smiling at Jacob again, who was tugging at her hand. Amy studied the table top.

"Perhaps," Mr Greenwood said. "It's best they tell you themselves."

Amy took a deep breath to steady her nerves, then looked up at her parents. Dad looked concerned. Mum's earlier jovial hospitality had been replaced by a questioning look, her frown suggesting that she was ready to convey disapproval.

"Well?" Dad asked.

Cat got your tongue? Amy guessed.

"Cat got your tongue?"

The familiarity of that was reassuring, something Amy could draw courage from. A surety to hang on to, as they headed off into unknown territory. She started speaking hesitantly. "There was a…I was on my way home…to the bus stop…there was a man…"

"On North Street," Mr Greenwood supplied. "In front of the Co-Op."

"Dad!" Frances protested. "You said to let us speak."

"Oh yes. I did. Sorry."

Amy looked her mum straight in her eyes, and said: "A homeless man."

She braced herself, but Mum remained calm, just echoing Amy's words tonelessly: "A homeless man."

"He was choking. Badly. He could barely breathe." The words came tumbling out now. "I called an ambulance. The ambulance men came. I went to the hospital as well."

"The Royal Sus..."

"Dad!"

"Sorry."

"You went to the hospital?" Amy's father asked. "Were you hurt?"

Amy shook her head. "They thought he was my father, so they let me ride in the ambulance."

"They thought what...?" Mum asked. "What did we tell you about homeless people? We told you not to..."

"Mum!" Amy interrupted. "I was just passing by, honest. I was on my way to the bus. He couldn't breathe!"

Mum shook her head firmly. "You're just a child, Amy, you have no business..."

"North Street is always busy," Dad said. "I'm sure there would have been plenty of people around."

"There were lots of people! But..."

"Then you should have let them handle it." Mum's face went into disapproval mode. "There's no call for you to..."

"NO!" Amy exclaimed. "You DON'T understand! You're NOT listening to me. Why can't you listen to me?"

Both Mum and Dad were visible taken aback by the anger in Amy's voice. Amy was shocked herself.

I've never ever spoken to them like this before.

Frances directed her attention at Jacob. Mr Greenwood fidgeted awkwardly with a teaspoon. Mum took a deep breath, but Dad beat her to it. "Go on," he said. "We'll listen."

"There were lots of people. But NONE of them stopped. NONE of them would help! I asked them. I begged them. I BEGGED people for help. And they all just looked away. Do you understand? They looked away, and then they walked away."

A wave of exhaustion hit Amy, and she slouched in her chair. She let her head drop and squeezed her eyes tightly shut.

"Unfortunately for Amy," Mr Greenwood said. "But fortunately for Gaz, the homeless man, Amy was far more adult than anybody else there."

"Grown-ups!" Frances added fiercely. "They did nothing." She reached over and squeezed Amy's hand.

"That may be…" Mum hesitated.

Mr Greenwood shook his head. "The long and short of it, Mr and Mrs Wheatley, is that your daughter saved a man's life today."

Amy gasped. She hadn't considered the afternoon's drama in this way. Nor had she heard it described in these strong terms.

All I did was call an ambulance.

"Saved a man's life?" Dad sounded astonished. Amy raised her head to see that surprise reflected on his face as well.

"It sounds like a big thing for a little girl to do…" Mr Greenwood started to say.

"Surely you exaggerate." Mum shook her head.

"Surely not," Mr Greenwood countered. "I spoke to Dr Sengupta at the Sussex, she's treating Gaz. Dr Sengupta told me very clearly that if Amy hadn't intervened…it would have been too late. Amy kept her head cool, and made the right decisions, when no one else would. Dr Sengupta was most insistent that Amy saved the man's life by her actions. Her behaviour this afternoon is something to be proud of. Very proud."

Amy blushed at the praise. She and Frances squeezed hands again. Jacob saw, and reached out his chubby little hand, looking up at his big sister full of concern. Amy was touched and gave him a warm smile, which seemed to reassure him, for he beamed and babbled something incomprehensible.

She looked at her parents. Both of them stared at Amy as if they had never seen her before.

"Why didn't you call us?" Mum asked at last. She sounded hurt.

"I tried to get in touch with Frances." Amy avoided the question. "But she didn't answer so I texted her."

"The Co-Op manager came outside when he noticed the commotion." Mr Greenwood said. "And he phoned me. Frances and I went to The Sussex immediately."

"Why would he phone..." Dad began, but Mum cut him short.

"But why didn't you call me?" Mum had disbelief in her eyes.

"I...I didn't..." Amy's voice trailed off.

"She was too scared." Frances blurted out. "She's afraid of you."

Mum looked like she had been punched. Her mouth dropped open.

"Frances...!" Mr Greenwood shook his head at Frances.

"It's true!" Frances insisted. She looked at Amy. "Tell them."

"Amy." Mum spoke quietly. "Is this true?"

Amy nodded, then swallowed as she saw something in her Mum break. "Mum, the other day, on London Road...you hurt my arm...you frightened me...you really hurt me..."

"Why didn't you tell me that then?"

"I did! But you weren't listening to me."

Amy felt tears welling up. She didn't want to cry. She tried to stop it. She was eleven-point-five. She had saved a man's life. She was...

...Something gave way. It felt as if she was collapsing like a house of cards scattered by the wind. She began to weep.

Through the blur of her tears, she saw Mum rise from her seat and circle the table. She walked hesitantly, almost in slow motion. Then Mum did what Amy yearned for, she opened her arms in invitation. Amy jumped up and found refuge in her mother's arms, holding on to her for dear life, sobbing as the tears flowed steadily.

"I'm so sorry...I'm so sorry..." Mum kept repeating.

112

"Amy? Whatmatter? Mummy?" Jacob's lip started trembling, but he was distracted when Frances gathered him up and pulled him onto her lap.

At long last, Amy and Mum untangled. Mum returned to her seat, wiping her eyes. Amy sat down again too, trembling, but feeling much better.

"What must you think of us?" Mum asked Mr Greenwood. "You must think I'm a terrible mother."

"No, Mrs Wheatley." Mr Greenwood shook his head. "I think that you wanted to protect your daughter, and believe you me, I fully understand that feeling." He looked at Frances for a moment, before he continued. "I've been in this business for eight years, and I am reminded daily of potential dangers. I'm very careful with Frances's involvement for that very reason."

"Hang on." Amy's father looked puzzled. "What business? What involvement?"

"There's more to this," Mr Greenwood said. "Than just Gaz choking on the street and the hospital today. I'm afraid these two haven't come out of this fray smelling entirely of roses, have you girls?"

He looked at them meaningfully, and both Amy and Frances shook their heads.

"Dad helps the homeless," Frances said. "Food, drink, clothes, sleeping bags..."

"He runs the Sunday Street Kitchen at the Clock Tower," Amy added.

Dad just stared. Mum shook her head, looking very tired. Amy knew how that felt, she was absolutely drained herself.

"*Sunday* Street Kitchen?" Mum asked.

"I'm sorry," Amy lowered her eyes. "I lied to you. I helped out there last Sunday."

"We lied," Frances admitted. "Sort of. Both of us."

Mum became cross, she looked at Mr Greenwood coldly. "Just because you make your daughter..."

"No!" Frances objected. "He doesn't *make* me do anything. I know that we're young, but eleven..."

Eleven-point-five.

"...is old enough to be able to tell right from wrong. I like the right, and I don't like the wrong. And Dad is trying to fix it. I help him because I *want* to."

Frances's outburst left Amy's parents flabbergasted. Amy covered her mouth to hide a smile, because the looks on their faces were almost comical.

"They've got minds of their own." Mr Greenwood shrugged apologetically. "Very inconvenient sometimes, I must admit. I would have preferred an exact clone of myself, but alas..."

That drew a laugh from Amy's father, but Mum narrowed her eyes. "You took our daughter to a street kitchen? With all those..."

"Homeless people," Mr Greenwood said firmly. "Some of them wrestling with their personal demons, but all of them well-behaved when I'm around."

"Nonetheless..." Mum began.

Mr Greenwood raised his hands. "I wouldn't have, if I had known your position on this. The girls neglected to tell you where I was taking them, and they forgot to tell me that you didn't know what we'd be doing. They played us for fools, and I am the biggest fool because I should have checked, to make sure. For that, I'm genuinely sorry, Mrs Wheatley, Mr Wheatley. I do apologise."

Mum looked at Amy, helplessly. "We didn't raise you..."

"I know. It was wrong. I am sorry," Amy said. She wanted to add a thousand things, explain, give reasons, justify...but what it boiled down to was that she had played with the truth, in a big way.

"I'm sorry too," Frances mumbled, with a guilty glance at her father.

Mr Greenwood cleared his throat. "I've made it very clear to both girls that I'm tremendously disappointed…"

Amy cringed. Disappointment was much worse than anger.

"And I will repeat my displeasure to Frances when we get home. At length. Including repercussions. I'm going to save a fortune not dishing out pocket money for a while, I reckon…"

"Aww, Dad!" Frances pouted.

"None of your wily ways, girl, not now," Mr Greenwood told her. "You put me in a rotten position, especially with Amy's parents."

Frances nodded guiltily.

Mr Greenwood looked at Amy's parents. "I only found out today, after we left the hospital. I wanted to speak to you anyway, after what Amy's been through today, but reckoned this needed to be talked about."

"Well," Amy's father replied. "We appreciate that, don't we?" He looked at Mum.

She hesitated, then said: "Yes, yes we do. I am sorry."

"There's one more concern I'd like to share," Mr Greenwood said. "And then we'll be on our merry way. I've got an errand to run, and this wayward child of mine no doubt expects to be fed."

Mr Greenwood took a deep breath, before he continued. "I've been more than worried about Frances lately."

"Who? Me?" Frances asked. "Why?"

"Yes, you. Since the start of this new school of yours, to be precise. When you came home from your old school, I could barely keep up with your happy chatter about the things you got up to at school. Ever since you've been going to this new school, you've come home grumpy, and mope for hours. Until you met Amy. Now you chatter again: Amy this, Amy that…"

Mr Greenwood looked at Amy and gave her a warm smile. Amy looked at Frances with surprise. She was aware of how important

Frances had become to her, but she hadn't realised that this had worked both ways.

Mr Greenwood turned to Amy's parents. "I'm sure you've made similar observations? I understand Amy was having a hard time in Year 7 as well."

"Nonsense," Mum said. "Amy has loads of friends."

"Jenny, Alima, Hope, Jasmin..." Dad started summing up. He looked at Amy as he did so, and she was startled by what she read in his eyes.

He knows now, he understands.

"Precisely," Mum said. "It's not as if we don't know our own daughter. We may have been a little busy lately..."

Dad put his hand on hers. "Nance. All of those were Amy's friends in primary school."

"It's...what?" Mum shut up, looked bewildered, and then embarrassed.

"How many friends from her new school has she talked about?" Dad asked. "Or brought home? We've been a bit blind, I think."

Mum looked uncomfortable, and seemed relieved when Mr Greenwood picked up his line of thinking again.

"What I'm getting at, is that I think it'd be a shame to obstruct this friendship. I fully understand that you don't want Amy at street kitchens, or the like. But if possible, other arrangements could be made? For the girls to spend time together?"

"Maybe I can still help baby-sit?" Frances asked in a very small voice.

Amy' parents exchanged a glance.

"I don't know..." Dad said. "I agree...but..."

"I appreciate that you've raised this, Mr Greenwood," Mum said. "But perhaps you can understand that we've taken on board a lot of information tonight," she paused. "Both commendable behaviour and less so, especially the lies. I need some time to digest all of this, and I'd like to talk about it with my husband first."

"I understand," Mr Greenwood nodded. "Thank you for the tea, I'm glad we've had a chance to clear the air."

"We'll be in touch," Dad said.

Amy sighed. She felt enormously relieved that it had all gone much better than she had expected, and she was still basking in the warmth of Mum's embrace, but Amy already hated the uncertainty of not knowing how it would end.

Frances and Mr Greenwood left.

Dinner was subdued that night. There were a few half-hearted attempts to talk about normal things, but these died down quickly, absorbed as everybody was in their thoughts.

Amy went to bed early. She felt hollow, depleted, exhausted. She lay in bed, and could hear the muffled voices of her parents in the living room below. They would be talking about it now. Amy worried that she'd be unable to sleep with all the thoughts jostling for attention in her mind, but when she closed her eyes, she was out like a light.

15. The Verdict in Fiveways

Amy's uncertainty was kept mercifully short.

When she came down for breakfast in the morning, it appeared that Mum and Dad had reached a conclusion.

"Only under adult supervision," Mum pronounced.

"I don't understand?"

"Frances is welcome to come here and help baby-sit Jacob, or just visit." Mum said. "And if you insist on helping these homeless people..."

Amy recalled Frances's words from the night before. "Mum, it's wrong, it's just wrong."

"I think we'll have to differ in opinion about that. But I'm willing to respect your opinion."

"...and listen to it." Dad added. "A bit more than ...well...huh...before."

"Thank you," Amy said.

"At school..." Mum said. "...I didn't know...I thought I had asked you now and then, how your day at school was."

"You did," Amy said quickly. "It's just that...you seemed..."

"Busy," Dad supplied.

Amy nodded. "They call me names."

"Names?" Mum frowned.

"Freckle Face...Ginger...that kind of stuff," Amy said.

"Well, you know what they say," Dad said. "Sticks and stones may break my bones..."

"But words will never hurt me," Amy completed. "But it's not true, Dad. The words do hurt. Also, it's more than just words, it's the whole...the way that people treat me."

"I have a mind to call your school," Mum said. "And get this sorted out."

"Don't!" Amy vividly recalled when the mother of the girl with braces had triggered a homeroom lecture on bullying. Their homeroom tutor had not mentioned the pupil's name, but she had foolishly given the girl a few too many meaningful looks so that everybody knew, and the girl's life had been made extra miserable for a few weeks.

"You'll just make it worse," Amy said.

"But…" Mum hesitated. "Yes, I suppose you're right. I recall something similar at school."

"You were bullied?" Amy asked, full of wonder.

Mum nodded, smiled sadly, and then indicated her hair, as red as Amy's. "I should have known, perhaps…"

"You're going to have to deal with the bullies somehow, Amy," Dad said. "You can't let them have it all their own way."

"I want to," Amy said. "I want it to stop. But how?"

Dad shrugged uncomfortably. "You should always stand up to bullies."

"Yes," Mum agreed. "You should always stand up to bullies. No matter what."

Maybe, but it's not very helpful. How?

"Well, I am," Amy said. "I mean, I have been standing up to them. Since I met Frances…together…"

Mum and Dad exchanged a glance.

"I think Frances is a lovely girl," Mum said. "A little headstrong perhaps…"

"You may be outmatched there, Amy," Dad quipped.

Amy smiled. She had felt some tension coming down the stairs earlier, unsure as to how her parents had taken it all in. This was nice though, they were talking to her on a different level than ever before, as if they had realised that eleven-point-five was old enough for some important things.

"I don't…" Mum glanced at Dad. "We don't entirely agree with what Mr Greenwood is doing, but he seemed very honest, and obviously cares for Frances. So we've decided that you can visit

Frances, and go along to this street kitchen, or wherever else Mr Greenwood works. Provided that he promises adult supervision at all times."

"We don't want you out there on your own," Dad said. "Or only with Frances. I'll call him and see if he agrees. I should think he will."

"You mean...I can go to the street kitchen? And The Office?"

"Provided that we know where you'll be," Dad said. "And when, and with whom, with Mr Greenwood or his staff there. No more fibs."

Amy shook her head, breathlessly.

"And be *careful*," Mum added sternly. "Stay out of trouble."

Amy nodded, "I promise! Thank you! Can I be excused?"

"May I be excused," Mum corrected. "Yes, you may. I suppose you will want to tell Frances about..."

Amy was already half-way up the stairs, racing for her room, her fingers flying across her phone screen. Frances answered the call just as Amy ran into her room and threw herself on her bed, greeting Frances by whooping jubilantly.

END OF PART TWO

PART THREE

16. A Coincidental Meeting at Pelham Square

After all of the drama of the previous day, it was hard to concentrate at school. The day seemed to last forever, until, at long last, the final bell signalled freedom. Amy and Frances found each other, and started walking off the school grounds. There was a vague plan to head into town for a few hours, but they hadn't agreed on a definite destination yet.

"I got a message from Dad," Frances said. "None of our people have seen Hailey today."

"Have they looked?"

"Yes, Dad drove up and down London Road a couple of times, he also checked out Providence Place and The Level. He said Tamara looked along the seafront and Old Steine, and Big John checked out New Road and the Pavilion Gardens."

"So we don't know if she knows about Gaz?" Amy pursed her lips. She knew that Hailey wasn't Gaz's girlfriend, nor family, but in a way they were like family. It only seemed right that Hailey was told. She might be really worried about Gaz if she couldn't find him, knowing he was ill.

Recalling recent events, Amy asked: "Has anybody checked Pelham Square?"

Frances snapped her fingers. "Bingo! No, I don't think so."

"Do you think…," Amy started saying.

"I'm not sure," Frances looked doubtful. "After yesterday and all…Dad really gave me an earful when we got home."

"I don't want to break the new rules," Amy said quickly. "But if we walk to North Laine…up Trafalgar Street…"

"…we'll pass by Pelham Square…"

"…We can see the park from the road…"

"...Just passing by."

"We'd walk there anyways..."

"...If we went to North Laine," Frances concluded.

"So how about we go to North Laine?" Amy asked.

"I thought you'd never ask," Frances answered, and they both laughed.

As they walked down into town, they discussed the previous day, including the emotionally loaded meeting around the Wheatley dinner table.

They had talked about it that morning, before the bell rang, but that had been in a rush, torrents of words hurling round like a whirl pool. Lunch had been better, they had managed to list everything that happened, but there had been little time to explore it in full. There was much to talk about, and before Amy knew it, they were already at York Place, opposite St Peter's. They took a right turn onto Trafalgar Street, and then ambled along the pavement, giggling at their attempts to look innocent as they approached Pelham Square as purely coincidental passer-by's.

"We should have sunglasses!" Frances said. "Spies always wear sunglasses."

"I wish I was wearing my hat," Amy said. "Sunglasses and hat, nobody would even recognise me."

They spotted Hailey almost immediately, leaning forward on the far bench in the park, elbows on knees, and clutching her head.

Amy and Frances exchanged an uncertain look.

"If..." Frances hesitated.

Amy knew why. They had made solemn promises, after having escaped through the eye of a needle. They hadn't really thought about it before, when they set up Amy's visit to the Sunday street kitchen. It had seemed mostly like innocent fun with a bit of guilt thrown in, but now things were pretty clear. This time, they knew there could be consequences, like not being allowed to see each other after school anymore. The thought of that alone…

Amy shrugged. "It's Hailey, and it doesn't look like she's feeling well. We ought to at least tell her about Gaz."

"Make sure she's okay," Frances agreed.

"It'd be rude not to say 'hello'," Amy added.

They entered the park, and cautiously approached Hailey, who was still cradling her head in her hands and staring at the ground.

Amy came to a stop when Frances did, at a careful distance.

"Hey Hailey," Amy said.

Hailey groaned.

"You okay?" Frances asked.

Hailey slowly raised her head. She looked terrible, sickly with red-rimmed eyes, her hair a tangled mess.

"Please, go away," she croaked.

Amy and Frances exchanged a worried glance.

"Hailey, it's us," Frances said. "Frances and Amy."

"I know," Hailey snapped, then dropped into a dull monotone. "Don't want you to see me like this. Not today."

Amy saw an empty vodka bottle lying on its side in the grass. There was a congealing puddle of sick between Hailey's shoes, stains on her clothes, and a hint of pungent odour in the air.

"I don't want you two to see me like this," Hailey repeated. "Please."

"Okay Hailey," Frances said. "We'll go. We just wanted to know if you knew about Gaz. He's in hospital."

Hailey barked a bitter laugh, and pointed at the vodka bottle. "Why do you think I gave in to that this morning?"

"He's going to be okay, the Doctor said," Frances added.

Hailey shook her head. "The thought of…I don't know what I'd do without…oh hell." She rubbed at her eyes furiously. "Thought I was all cried out."

"Have you been to see Gaz?" Amy asked.

Hailey stared at her dully. "See him?"

"They have visiting hours at the hospital," Amy said. "You could, maybe, visit Gaz. I'm sure he'd like that."

"Don't be daft, girl," Hailey growled. "Do you think they'd let me inside, looking as I do?"

Amy shrugged, then said softly: "Maybe it's worth a try."

"Let's put it this way," Frances said. "Hailey, do you want to see Gaz?"

"I told you...they're not going to let..."

"But do you *want* to see him?" Frances persisted.

A tear rolled down Hailey's cheek. "Of course, of course I want to see him."

"That's good, then you will." Frances said. She fished her phone out of her coat pocket, and tapped the screen.

"Hey Dad," she said cheerfully. "I need adult supervision. We're at Pelham Square. Hailey is here, she's..."

Frances paused, and rolled her eyes. "No, no Dad, we weren't. Amy and I were on our way to North Laine. We passed and saw...No Dad. Honest, we were just passing. Hailey is in a bad way, she's very upset about Gaz...That's what we said, but she says they won't let her in, she needs a wash and some clean clothes."

Frances spent some time listening, and flashed Amy a thumbs-up.

"Okay, Dad. We'll do that...Right, see you in a minute."

Frances put the phone away.

Amy asked: "Is he coming here?"

"Your dad?" Hailey asked.

"He'll be here soon," Frances explained. "Amy and I going to go meet him up the road, he's there for an errand, and then we'll come back here with the van."

Hailey plucked at her stained clothes.

"We'll go to The Office. There's a shower there, and clean clothes," Frances promised.

"Hospital visiting hours?" Hailey asked.

"I dunno," Frances answered. "But Dad'll get you in, and you'll get to see Gaz. Will you stay put? We won't be long."

"I'll stay," Hailey said, then smiled sadly. "Got nowhere else to go. Thank you."

"Come on," Frances beckoned Amy. "Let's go see Miss Puck at The Owlery."

"Miss Puck!?"

17. The Owlery on Kemp Street

They made their way up Trafalgar Street, Frances grinning happily as Amy badgered her about Miss Puck, but refusing to supply any more information.

"You'll see," She kept on repeating.

Amy recalled that Miss Puck had mentioned something about a shop, that afternoon at the street kitchen, and supposed that this was where they were going. She wondered what kind of shop someone like Miss Puck would run, and peered into each new set of shop windows as they progressed up the street, but none seemed to fit.

"Is it a clothes shop?" She asked, recalling Miss Puck's eccentric outfit.

"You'll see," Frances answered.

"A pet shop?" Amy recalling talk of owls.

"You'll see," Frances answered.

"Books then! It must be a book shop."

"You're getting warmer." Frances grinned. "But not just books."

"You'll see."

"Aargh!"

When turned the corner onto Kemp Street, she recognized the image on the old-fashioned shop sign hanging from a bracket over the shop door. It was the same picture that was on the business card Miss Puck had given her, with Thallie the barn owl and the name *The Owlery*. Green wood panelling surrounded windows which were bright with warm golden light. Amy gasped when she saw the items neatly presented in the window displays.

"Well?" Frances asked, looking pleased.

"Can we go in?" Amy could barely wait to explore.

Frances grinned. "Yeah, we're meeting my dad in here."

They pushed through the door. The shop was small, but filled from top to bottom with a treasure trove. A polished wood display cabinet held dozens of crystal balls, large and small, as well as figurines of Pooks, Wyrms, owls, ferrets, or familiar *Secrets of the Wyrde Woods* characters such as tall Walking Tree, the armoured Lewinna and the elegantly robed Niada. One display case had jewellery, silver gleaming bright, with images and symbols of the Wyrde Woods or old Sussex myths. Amy spotted the Silver Swan hanger, so intricately beautiful that her mouth dropped open. She also marvelled at a replica of Niada's silver dagger. There was a case full of books, all the Wyrde Woods books, including the illustrated ones. Framed artwork decorated the walls, depicting scenes from the novels. Best of all, another display table contained dozens of magical wands, neatly written labels attached to all of them.

"I think I've died and gone to heaven!" Amy said. "It's like...it's like walking into The Wyrde Woods."

"I knew you would like it!" Frances beamed.

Miss Puck was at the far end of the shop, behind an old fashioned wooden shop counter, rows and rows of shelves behind her, laden with glass pots filled with sweets and candy.

"Welcome to The Owlery, young witches," she announced brightly.

"Hey Miss Puck," Frances greeted her cheerfully.

"Young Miss Frances!" Miss Puck's face, already drawn in cheer, beamed with delight. He looked at Amy, "and the very talented young artist from the Clock Tower!"

"I'm Amy."

"I am honoured by your visit, Amy."

"I didn't know..." Amy indicated the shop around her. "This was here..."

"I've only recently opened," Miss Puck told her. "Do you like it?"

"It's...magical," Amy said.

Miss Puck clasped her hands together. "Then I've succeeded! Did you know the author lives in Brighton?"

"Really?"

"Yes, he's dropped by a couple of times. Said he couldn't believe it."

"I can well imagine!" Amy cast half a glance at the shop's door, half hoping the author would walk in. The next book in the series was long overdue.

Miss Puck turned to Frances. "Now Miss Greenwood, what brings you here on this cold winter's day?"

"I was feeling a bit peckish," Frances said hopefully.

"Oh you were, were you?" Miss Puck winked, and placed her index finger along the length of her nose.

"Starving, actually," Frances said. "So's Amy. We'll probably faint any minute now."

"Well, we can't have that, young witches require ample feeding." Miss Puck reached for one of the jars behind her, and fished out two pieces of chocolate shaped in the form of owls.

Amy shook her head, "I haven't got any..."

"Consider it payment,"Miss Puck said. "For your hard work at the Clock Tower."

Frances wasted no time, said a hurried "Thank you" and then but into her owl with relish.

Amy was slower, admiring the owl first, before trying the chocolate which was sweet and crunchy.

"Now don't you go telling anybody I've been generous," Miss Puck said. "I'll have half of Brighton on my doorstep tomorrow morning hoping for a chocolate owl, including the author who says he's impoverished. I'm no Uncle Scrooge, but it would ruin my business!"

The girls shook their heads.

"I was hoping your father would drop by." Miss Puck told Frances.

"He's on his way," Frances answered between bites. "He asked us to meet him here."

"Excellent!" Miss Puck exclaimed happily. "A remarkable man!"

"Why is he coming here?" Amy wondered.

"Ah!" Miss Puck retrieved an envelope from beneath the counter, and tapped it on the counter's top. "Treasure! Gleaming doubloons, golden florins and silver shillings."

"Miss Puck donates some of the shop's money to Dad," Frances said.

"Oh!" Amy exclaimed. "That's very kind of you."

"It's the least I can do," Miss Puck explained. "I live in Brighton, and I make my living in Brighton. I see all of those unfortunate people on the pavement, or in shop doorways, when I walk on Brighton streets, but don't know how to best help them."

Amy nodded.

"But I want to do something, to do my bit. So I help out Tom Greenwood, because he is something else, isn't he? Every penny I give to him is spent far more wisely than any of the many tax pounds I have to give to the government."

Another customer came in, to be greeted in jubilant style by Miss Puck, and Frances pulled Amy to the side.

"You've got chocolate around your mouth," Amy told her friend.

Frances wiped her mouth. "Isn't it slick here?"

"It's lit," Amy agreed.

The girls wandered over to the magic wand display and began to browse. Amy had bought a wand once, at one of the cheap stores on London Road, but it had never really been anything more than a lump of brightly coloured plastic, with sharp mould lines which hurt her hand when she held it. Miss Puck's wands were something different altogether. They were beautifully crafted from real wood, and when Amy held them, she was pleasantly surprised to note the weight of them. These didn't feel like cheap toys at all.

"It's like they're real!" She marvelled. Frances nodded her agreement.

"Hand-crafted by an old-timer in the Weald." Miss Puck briefly broke off her conversation with the new customer. "Finds the branches himself, swears the time to do so is at night during a full moon."

They waved the wands around, and Amy repeated some Wyrde Woods spells she recalled. Then they started selecting their favourite wands, and narrowed the list down until they both arrived at their first and foremost choice.

Behind them the shop door opened, and Mr Greenwood's voice filled the shop. "Every time I come here, I smile," he announced. "How can anybody not smile in here?"

The other customer left again, and Miss Puck greeted Mr Greenwood heartily. The envelope exchanged hands, and Mr Greenwood thanked Miss Puck profusely.

"We'll see it put to good use," he promised.

"I know," Miss Puck said. "That is why I am giving it to you, and nobody else."

"Thank you. Much obliged." Mr Greenwood turned to the girls. "So. As I understand it, you accidentally passed Pelham Square, and then coincidentally saw Hailey. How very fortuitous. I know it must have been a fluke, because after yesterday's agreements..."

"It might have been magical," Miss Puck suggested.

Mr Greenwood chuckled, but Frances slipped into her serious mode.

"She's in a bad state, Dad. Took the news badly, she'd been drinking."

"She said she would be lost without Gaz," Amy added.

"I can well imagine." Mr Greenwood frowned. "Is she still drunk?

Frances shook her head. "No, Dad, you know I wouldn't get close and talk if she was. But, she's not feeling well, and she looks like something General dragged into The Office."

"Oh dear," Miss Puck said.

"I think it would help her, Mr Greenwood, to visit Gaz," Amy dared to suggest.

Mr Greenwood looked at her thoughtfully for a moment. "It prolly would, and it would be good for Gaz as well."

"But we couldn't take her on our own," Frances added. "That's why I called for adult supervision. As agreed."

Mr Greenwood shifted his gaze to her, and said nothing.

Frances coloured red.

Mr Greenwood shook his head wearily. "Right, we'll get the van, collect Hailey, take her to The Office, get her cleaned up, order something to eat, and then all visit the Sussex, to cheer up Gaz."

"Visiting hours are until eight," Amy said, for she had googled it. She felt disappointment welling up inside her. "But...I have to..."

"There is an advantage, to being honest," Mr Greenwood said, giving Frances a pointed look. He found his phone, tapped on his screen, and held the phone to his ear.

"Hello Josh, Tom here."

Amy marvelled at hearing Mr Greenwood address her dad in this familiar way.

"The girls would like to visit the man Amy saved at the hospital. I've a mind to take them this evening after dinner. Would you mind if Amy ate with us and came along? I'll drop her off home after...around eight."

Frances nudged Amy, who nudged back.

"Shiny! Thank you, Josh."

Mr Greenwood put his phone away. "Well that's arranged."

"You didn't mention Hailey to Amy's dad," Frances said slyly.

Her father took a deep breath. "I didn't want to complicate matters."

"But you're setting an example," Frances admonished him, "to impresson…impressin…"

"Impressionable," Miss Puck supplied helpfully.

"Impressionable young girls," Frances finished triumphantly.

"She's a sharp one, Tom," Miss Puck said. "As clever as they come."

"Too clever by half," Mr Greenwood sighed dramatically, and they all laughed at that.

18. Pizza and a Frank Talk at Crowhurst Road

Mr Greenwood called Tamara, when Amy and Frances helped Hailey into the van at Pelham Square.

"Tamara, Tom here. Are you at The Off...oh, you just left. I'm really sorry about this, but could you head back? I'm bringing in Hailey, she'll need a wash and clean clothes...thanks Tamara, you're a saint, so you are."

Tamara was waiting by the front door of The Office when they arrived. She looked very tired, but greeted Hailey with a smile, and ushered her up the stairs and into the depths of the labyrinth of rooms and corridors. Amy and Frances followed Mr Greenwood into the main office.

"I'm going to order our traditional Office meal, Amy, it's healthy and nutritious," Mr Greenwood declared.

"PIZZA!" Frances cheered.

After Mr Greenwood had ordered pizzas, he leaned back in his chair and shook his head. "And there I was, hoping for a quiet night in."

"You always say that," Frances commented dismissively. "Dad, Tamara looked really tired, do you think it was fair to ask her to come back?"

Mr Greenwood sighed, and it wasn't a theatrical sigh this time. "Sit down, the both of you."

Amy and Frances pulled up chairs. Mr Greenwood leant forwards, folding his hands between his knees, and looked at the girls earnestly.

"You both want to be taken seriously, which is prolly good, I suppose. So I'm going to have a little grown-up talk with you, and I want you to consider what I have to say carefully, okay?"

The girls nodded.

"It's also to stay between us," Mr Greenwood continued. "Understood?"

The girls nodded again.

"Right." Another deep sigh. "There are people in this city, who don't like what I do."

"The Council?" Frances asked.

"I'm not sure," Mr Greenwood answered. "I can only guess. I know some people genuinely believe that I am encouraging hordes of homeless to come to Brighton."

"That's ridiculous," Frances declared.

"So it is," Mr Greenwood agreed. "They are not paying attention. This homeless crisis is happening all over the country. Local authorities failing to help is happening all over the country. People are dying on the streets all over the country, especially during the winter months. And there are people like me in almost every city, trying to help. It's not as if people are coming to Brighton intentionally because Tom Greenwood will give them a bowl of chili and rice."

He paused for a moment, then continued. "Whoever it is, they certainly find a listening ear at the Council. There are some, I suspect, who'd like to close this whole operation down."

"No!" Amy called out.

"I'm afraid so, and that means that I have to be careful. And sometimes, that means I have to rely on Tamara, or some of the other volunteers."

Mr Greenwood stared at the floor for a moment, before looking up at them again. "It wouldn't do, for me to take a possibly drunk, vulnerable young woman to The Office in the evening, and get her into a shower. Tamara knows that, she understands and she doesn't mind. People talk, and some like saying nasty things about others. Do you two understand that?"

Amy didn't entirely, but then she thought back to that moment at the hospital, when the nurse had been so suspicious because she had assumed Amy had been hanging around in the company of Gaz. She also recalled that creepy man at the Clock Tower, in the beige raincoat, who offered homeless women a place to stay but wanted things from them. The thought that Mr Greenwood would take advantage of anybody at all seemed foolish to her, but not everybody knew what kind of man he was. She supposed that people who didn't know any better could be suspicious if they found out Mr Greenwood had taken Hailey to The Office after dark, with no one else around.

She answered, "Yes, I understand."

"I do too," Frances said.

"It's called safeguarding. That is also why I was so determined to talk about all of this with Amy's parents yesterday. And why I need the both of you to think carefully about your actions, even if it's for the benefit of a Hailey, or any of the others. Imagine that Amy came with us, but her parents didn't know, and reported her missing to the police? It wouldn't take them long, I reckon, to put two and two together, and visit the Clock Tower, or The Office, to find me in the company of a missing child."

"But…" Amy shook her head. "You wouldn't…it wouldn't be like that at all…"

"No," Mr Greenwood smiled sadly. "But some people would happily splash it out on the front page of *The Argus*. I really need you two to understand that."

"I understand," Frances said.

"So do I," Amy added. "I think it's unfair though."

"A lot of things are unfair," Mr Greenwood answered. "We either grow numb from it all and stop resisting, or we can do our best to fight it."

"I'll fight!" Frances volunteered.

Mr Greenwood smiled and ruffled her hair. "I never doubted that, but fight using this." He tapped the side of his head with his index finger. "Think first, then act. Not the other way around."

Frances nodded. Mr Greenwood looked at Amy. "How about you, Amy?"

She smiled. "Think first, then act."

"Shiny," Mr Greenwood got up. "I'd better go downstairs with some money, the pizza will be here soon. Frances, if you and Amy could select some books for Gaz? He likes reading, right?"

"Yes, he does," Amy said. "Thrillers, and detectives."

"Good, find him some books, we'll take them to the Sussex."

19. Reunion at Edward Street

Mr Greenwood didn't make it to Gaz's room straight away. He was stopped in a corridor, by a doctor, and told of new cases of malnutrition.

"Working families," the Doctor said, with a tired sigh. "Having to choose between paying their rent and bills, or feeding their children."

"These are hard times we live in," Mr Greenwood answered. "I can put them down for a standard weekly food package, and one of us can visit to see if there's anything else they need. Sometimes there'll be broken down appliances, not enough clothes for the kids..."

"...or toys." Frances added. "We do those too."

The Doctor was grateful, and asked Mr Greenwood to come to his office to note down the contact details.

"Go on and see Gaz," Mr Greenwood told the others. "I'll be right along."

Frances asked: "Dad, what about the adult supervision thing?"

Mr Greenwood shook his head in exasperation, then looked at Hailey. Amy followed his gaze. The blemishes on Hailey's face were fading memories. She was all cleaned up, her hair combed and showing a lively shine. Tamara had found some old clothes amongst the donations at The Office. Instead of her usual boots, combat trousers and fleece, Hailey was wearing formal clothes: a proper skirt, a blouse and a short jacket. The transformation was remarkable.

"How are you feeling, Hailey?" Mr Greenwood asked.

"Almost human," she answered with a smile.

"You don't fool me." Mr Greenwood chuckled. "Reckon you can properly supervise these two rascals?"

Hailey looked at the girls. "Can I devise cruel and unusual punishments if they misbehave?"

"Absolutely," Mr Greenwood promised. "Very well, I hereby promote you to Temporary Adult Supervisor, it's voluntary work, but a very responsible task. Proper VIP stuff."

"Sounds good, thanks Tom."

Amy and Frances followed Hailey down the corridor, Mr Greenwood and the doctor headed off in a different direction.

"I don't mind," Frances whispered to Amy. "But he's cheating a little bit. Especially after that talk at the office, about using your brains and stuff."

Amy looked at Hailey walking in front of them. There was nothing about her this evening that indicated Hailey was anything other than a regular visitor, come to see a relative or friend.

"Maybe he thinks it's different here," Amy replied. "Because we're in a hospital, not on London Road or anything."

Hailey stopped walking. She turned around. "Do you two reckon I ain't capable of a bit of adult responsibility then?"

"Nothing to do with you Hailey," Frances said. "It's about Dad."

"Well I like it," Hailey declared. "It means he trusts me with you, and that's a big compliment from Tom Greenwood. Especially after the way I was in the park earlier."

Her smile faded. "It don't make me feel anything better about the park. I wish you hadn't seen me in that state. I'm sorry."

Amy said the first thing on her mind: "You're looking really pretty now."

"Thanks," Hailey smiled. "Tamara gave me street gear too, it's in the van. I'll put it on...after. But it's a good feeling. Out there, you forget what it's like sometimes, you forget what it is like to be..."

"Human," Amy said.

"Yeah, human." Hailey answered. "Anyways, I'm sorry about earlier. And thank you. For all this. It may all seem really simple to you, but it's a big step for me."

"No problem." Frances said.

"I think Gaz's room is just at the end of this corridor." Amy pointed.

"Betcha he ain't expecting me!" Hailey sounded genuinely happy. "Let's go surprise him."

They crowded in the doorway, to see Gaz lying in a hospital bed. Hailey said: "Wazzup, Gaz?"

The look on his face was priceless. Amy and Frances grinned happily.

"Not much, kiddo," Gaz replied, when he had recovered from his astonishment. "I barely recognised you, come marching in looking all respectable."

His voice was weak, he looked pale and gaunt. He was clearly still ill, but not in the alarming manner Amy had seen at the North Street Co-Op. He was calm, and seemed reasonably at ease.

Hailey crossed the room and pulled up a chair by Gaz's bed.

Amy and Frances approached the bed as well.

"Hey, Gaz," Frances said. "We brought you some books."

She placed the paperbacks she was carrying on his bedside table.

"That's mighty considerate of you." Gaz smiled. "Thank you, Frances."

He looked at Amy. "They told me what you did," he said softly. "I don't even know how to begin to thank you."

Amy shrugged awkwardly.

Hailey took Gaz's hand into her own, and gave Amy a warm look. "She saved your life, Gaz."

"I know," Gaz said. He closed his eyes briefly. When he opened them again, Amy could see that they were moist, and his voice trembled a little when he spoke: "Most people...so few people..."

He shook his head wearily, and Hailey squeezed his hand.

Amy wasn't sure how to respond to Gaz's emotions. They seemed to be contagious, because she could feel an intense sadness threatening to overwhelm her. She bit on her lip. It wouldn't do to cry, she reckoned, she'd cried plenty already.

She was sure that there was probably something important to say, something suitable for the gravity of the occasion, but all she could manage was: "I'm glad you're starting to feel better."

"I am," Gaz agreed. "Have you two dealt with those bullies at school yet?"

Amy and Frances shared a quick glance. Word at school was that the Trolls had sworn revenge, and were planning all sorts of horrible things. So far, Amy and Frances had managed to evade them, but they knew that couldn't last forever.

"Not yet," Frances answered lightly. "It won't be a problem."

"Oh?" Gaz raised an eyebrow.

"We'll manage," Amy assured him.

"I suppose you'll have to," Gaz said. He turned to Hailey. "Has SWEP been activated yet? It's still cold outside, isn't it?"

"Bloody freezing," Hailey answered. "But no SWEP yet. I've been kipping around North Laine."

She started to give Gaz the news from the streets. New people who had drifted into town, old people who had drifted out, more confiscations of people's backpacks and sleeping bags, and the eviction of two small tent camps.

Amy watched them talk. It was odd to see Hailey and Gaz indoors like this. It seemed so normal, and was at odds with Amy's knowledge that the two had no home to call their own, nor a safe and warm place to sleep at night. More than ever, Amy felt the strong conviction that it just wasn't right.

"Well, well, well." Mr Greenwood entered the room. "Not dead yet?"

Gaz gave him a weak grin, and shook his head. "They can't get rid of me that easily, Tom. I've got some reading to do first." He indicated the books on his bedside table. "Kind of worried about Hailey though. Do you know what's going on with SWEP?"

"We've got people phoning Councillors, and sending E-mails," Mr Greenwood answered. "Council says they've outsourced it to Brighton Housing Trust, and that it isn't their call. BHT says they've got to stick to the national guidelines, but that some Council people can overrule these based on common sense, especially regarding the wind chill factor. BHT said that they were ready to open up First Base, eager to do so even, but they're bound by protocol and are waiting for a green light from the Council."

"Common sense from the Council," Gaz said slowly. "Uh-oh."

"Uh-oh, indeed," Mr Greenwood said. "Not a job requirement there, apparently. Dr Worthley has written the Council a letter, specifying the dangers of the wind chill, spelling out that lives are at stake, but hey-ho, it's the usual: 'What do medical experts know about health matters?'"

"Good grief." Gaz shook his head sadly.

"And while they bicker who is responsible," Hailey said, with bitterness in her voice. "We're left out on the streets to die."

"Not if I can help it," Mr Greenwood growled. "Not on my watch. We're doing night runs now. Hot drinks, extra sleeping bags. Responding to information people call through to us, when they've seen someone having a bad time of it."

"But it's so cold outside! Can't they just open a building somewhere?" Amy asked.

"The funny thing is," Mr Greenwood said. "That they voted to do just that, at the end of last winter. Open a winter shelter. Just about the time they got a big extra lump of money from the government to tackle homelessness, over two million pounds."

"Two million pounds!" Amy couldn't even begin to imagine just how much money that was.

"You'd think," Gaz said. "That nine months and two million pounds should be sufficient to organise...something, at least."

"Yeah, you'd think that." Mr Greenwood nodded. "But we're not professionals, I'm continuously told, and professionals know better."

"How far have they got?" Hailey asked. "These professionals?"

Mr Greenwood shook his head. "Apparently they started a serious search for a building in mid-November."

"Mid-November!" Hailey's eyes widened. "But that's just a couple of weeks ago."

"We sent letters and emails in the spring, summer, and autumn," Mr Greenwood said. "Warning them that winter usually follows autumn, and winter has been known to be cold on occasion. Might as well have been howling at the moon, for all the good it did. And now they've been caught out by this current cold spell, and nobody wants to take responsibility."

"That's just horrible," Amy said.

"Disgusting," Frances added.

"Exactly," Mr Greenwood agreed. "I just hope they get their act together soon, before it's too late."

20. Shock in Hollingbury

It felt as things were settling down, falling into a pattern.

Frances came over on Saturday afternoon, to help mind Jacob. The girls played loud music and danced after Amy's parents left. Jacob loved every minute of it, stomping his little legs up and down, and hollering nonsense whenever the girls sang along to a refrain. Frances stayed for dinner that night, after which they watched a movie before Mr Greenwood came to pick Frances up.

On Sunday Amy went to help at the Clock Tower Street Kitchen. Although it was only her second time, she already found herself becoming part of the clockwork precision with which the mini-market was set up and operated. Clare made them tea. Hailey greeted them warmly. Tamara gossiped with Frances. Mrs Harwood stuffed her pockets full of biscuits. Little John came round for second, third, and fourth helpings. Big John made a point of formally shaking Amy's hand, telling her what a great job she'd done on North Street.

After the Street Kitchen, they all headed back to The Office.

"No child labour today," Mr Greenwood said, as they approached the industrial estate.

"YAY!" Frances cheered.

"Tamara has cleared the big desk for you." Mr Greenwood grinned. "So a couple of hours of homework, methinks."

"Dad, that's worse! Torture!"

"Duly noted."

That evening, Dad showed interest in the street kitchen, and asked questions about it. Mum refrained from making disparaging remarks, and Amy didn't know what she liked better, Dad's interest or Mum's diplomatic silence.

Even school seemed better somehow, on Monday. There were still Trolls to avoid, and the popular kids in Amy's class continued to play their stupid games, but Amy felt stronger, more confident. She shrugged off the occasional remarks about her hair, made it clear that she didn't really care what they thought, and that seemed to take the fun out of it for her nastier classmates.

She met with Frances before the first bell, and during every minute of break time. After the last bell they rushed to the gate to pile into Mr Greenwood's van, and he took them to The Office. He had prepared little lists for them, about the new families they were supporting. For each family, he had written down how many children there were, as well as their ages. Frances guided Amy deep into the storage areas, to reveal a room full of toys, and they had great fun selecting what they thought would be fitting toys for the kids in the new families.

On Tuesday morning, before the first bell, Amy greeted Frances with the question: "What are we going to do this afternoon?"

Whatever they were going to plan, Amy was already looking forward to it.

Frances's face fell. "I've got to go home after school, to take care of Dad."

"Is he ill?!"

Frances shook her head. "He's been up all night. Right until dawn. Oh, Amy, it's bad news, you're not going to like it."

"What's happened?"

"Gaz was discharged from the hospital, last night."

"Discharged? But on Sunday Hailey said that he's still not feeling well!"

"Dad said they don't have enough beds, or staff. That he's officially well enough to complete his recovery at home."

"But he doesn't have a home!"

"I know," Frances said in a small voice. "So he went back out onto the street, but nobody knows where he is, not even Hailey

Dad and some of the others were out all night, looking for him. Dad's asleep now, I want to be there when he wakes up, make him a cup of tea, some breakfast."

"Of course," Amy said. "Oh! I hope Gaz'll be alright. I just don't believe they would do such a thing."

She was alternatively angry and worried during the morning lessons, barely able to focus on the teachers.

Amy was one of the first ones out of the classroom at the beginning of lunch break, and went looking for Frances straight away. She found her friend in a hallway, her back toward Amy, and texting on her phone. She was shaking like a leaf.

"Frances?" Amy experienced a weird sinking feeling in her tummy, mixed with anxious concern for her friend.

Frances turned around to face Amy. Her cheeks were wet with tears, her eyes wild. "Oh Amy! They found him. They found Gaz. He's dead. Gaz is dead."

No. No. No. No.

21. Escape from Hollingbury

Amy and Frances retreated into the nearby girl's toilet. The cubicles were all empty, they were alone.

Frances told Amy the little that she knew. The body had been found in the upper reaches of the Preston Park Rock Gardens that morning.

No, no, no. We were talking to him just the other day, he was getting better.

"Dad is still asleep, I think," Frances sobbed. "I found out because Big John and Tamara were talking about it in a Street Kitchen whatsapp group. I don't think they realised I'm in that group."

"It could be a mistake. It has to be a mistake. It might be someone else."

It has to be someone else.

Frances shook her head. "It was Big John who found him and called 999."

Amy stared blindly at the tiled wall. She could feel tears welling up, and then running down her cheeks. "It can't be true, it has to be someone else."

"Amy! I just told you, Big John found him. He knows Gaz well enough. Gaz and…"

The girls looked at each other in shock, and then said simultaneously: "Hailey!"

The hallway door swung open, multiple footsteps indicating they had company, but Amy barely registered this, her mind on Hailey.

"Oh my God, Frances, Hailey is going to…"

"WE GOT YOU NOW, YOU LITTLE BITCHES!"

The girls spun around to see the three Trolls walk in. They were grinning fiendishly. The last one shut the door.

"Look at their faces. The little cry-babies have been bawling."

"No," Amy shook her head at them. "Not now, somebody has died."

"Shut up, Freckle Face!"

"I'll tell you who's gonna die, and that is your smelly friend Snowflake!"

"After we've held her head in a toilet pot and flushed!"

"Right where she belongs, with the other turds."

"I tell you what, Ginger Freak. You get the hell outta here now, we just want to flush Snowflake. Walk away or we'll do the same to you."

Amy shook her head furiously. "Didn't you hear me. Somebody's died."

"Oh boo-hoo."

"Was it one of your junkie friends?"

A red haze filled Amy's vision. "GAZ WAS NOT A JUNKIE!"

"One more dead addict, as if anybody cares."

"Grab them! Time to wash their filthy hair."

One of the Trolls advanced on Amy, who surprised herself with the calmness that she felt. In any other circumstance, she would have been terrified, but now she was just angry. Gaz was dead...

...*no, no, no...*

...Gaz was dead. Hailey was going to take it bad. That was real life. Not these stupid Trolls and their endless bullying.

Remember what Hailey said: kick 'em where it hurts.

Amy did just that. She knew that boys just about died from pain if you kicked them between the legs, she wasn't sure about girls —no-one had ever kicked her there— so she kicked as hard as she possibly could. There was a blurry streak to her side, Frances rushing forward, just as the tip of Amy's shoe made contact.

The Troll screamed and doubled over.

Good!

Another Troll yelped in pain, clutching her cheek "She bit me! That little bitch bit me!"

Frances grinned wolfishly.

Amy and Frances turned to the remaining Troll, who backed up against the wall.

Frances advanced, and raised her fists.

"No, no, don't," The Troll held up her empty hands. "Stop! Please."

Frances looked disgusted, and lowered her hands again. "Not so brave on your own, are you?"

"We'll remember that," Amy promised. She cast a look around. The Troll she had kicked, was curled up on the floor, sobbing. The Troll Frances had bit, was standing by a sink, splashing cold water on her cheek, and looking into the mirror with a horrified expression on her face.

Amy shook her head in disbelief. In just a few seconds, all the fight had gone out of the Trolls.

"Come on, Amy, we'd better go," Frances said, and tugged at Amy's hand.

Amy nodded. Although it didn't look like it, the Trolls might recover their senses. Then it'd be three against two again, and they were much bigger, and would be more wary now.

The two girls fled into the hallway.

"Where to?" Amy asked, not knowing any logical destination that would be safe, barely able to think.

Gaz is dead.

"Anywhere but here," Frances answered. "I just want to get out of school now. Off the school grounds too."

Amy nodded, feeling much the same. "We should go find Hailey."

"I want to," Frances bit her lip. "But you know we're not supposed to..."

"I don't care," Amy said stubbornly. "We almost got our heads stuck the toilets just now. That's not supposed to happen either. Gaz is dead. That wasn't supposed to happen. Besides, Hailey is our friend."

Frances wiped away a tear, then nodded her agreement. "Let's get the hell out of here."

22. Trolls on The Level

Amy and Frances rushed downtown in a single-minded hurry. They wanted to find Hailey. Nothing else mattered.

Amy vaguely registered that they were skiving off school. This might mean trouble, but she didn't care. If they stayed at school, they would probably get a beating from the Trolls, who would be out to get even.

Epic as the confrontation in the loos had been, it faded into insignificance next to the morning's bad news.

Gaz is dead.

Did Hailey know? Amy's mind conjured up the image of Hailey when they had visited Gaz in hospital. She had looked beautiful.

Almost human.

Then there was the Hailey they'd seen at Pelham Square: Broken, on the verge of giving up, bereft of all her dignity.

That first Hailey, the vibrant —almost human— one, was cause for hope, reason to believe that her circumstances were just temporary, with light at the end of the tunnel.

The second, a stark reminder of what could also happen if Hailey spent too much time drowning her sorrows in cheap vodka.

What would Hailey do when she heard about Gaz?

Gaz is dead.

Amy and Frances reached London Road. It didn't take Frances long to spot a rough sleeper whom she trusted, near the Cowley Club.

"Jimmy," she said, and the man looked up. He was elderly with sharp blue eyes, closely cropped grey hair and a trimmed white beard. His clothing was clean and neat. The only thing that gave him away as a rough sleeper was the sleeping bag he sat in.

"Hi Frances," Jimmy said. He gave Amy a friendly nod which she returned. "Shouldn't you two be in school?"

Frances didn't answer his question. "We're looking for Hailey. It's important, have you seen her?"

"Hailey?" Jerry scratched his head. "I saw her earlier, with Little John in tow; they said they were headed for The Level." He frowned. "She seemed upset about something."

"The Level!" Frances said.

"Upset..." Amy echoed.

She's found out already.

Amy and Frances negotiated their way across the busy London Road pavements, and then broke into a run as they headed up Baker Street. A man with a greying short-clipped beard and working man's cap, smoking a roll-up outside of the Cascade Coffee shop, commented on the girl's urgency as they passed.

"Such a hurry! There's always tomorrow."

The park was close. All they had to do at the end of Baker Street was cross Ditchling Road. They waited impatiently for the lights to turn green, apprehension growing.

What if she's drinking when we find her?

Amy glanced at Frances's face, which was set in determination. The expression on her friend's face was reassuring. At least this time Amy wouldn't be alone, as she had been on North Street.

The Level was busy, especially the large skating park, where many were performing derring-do acrobatics on roller skates and skate boards.

"There," Amy pointed at a bench, about halfway along the length of The Level. She might not have recognised Hailey straight away at this distance, for the tell-tale red hair had been tucked into a woollen cap, but Little John's hulking green form was unmistakable.

Frances came to an abrupt halt. "Uh-oh," she said. "Trouble."

Amy was puzzled by the remark. As far as she could tell both Hailey and Little John were calm. Hailey was speaking intently, Little

John nodding or shaking his head in response. There were no abrupt, uncontrolled movements, or any other signs to indicate drinking.

Then Amy saw four uniformed people, three men and a woman, approaching the pair on the bench. They wore bright yellow jackets with some sort of insignia and official looking stripes on them, as well as peaked caps.

"Police?" Amy asked, not sure because there was a vague resemblance to police officers, but it didn't seem quite the same.

"Public Safety Enforcement Officers," Frances answered. When she saw that Amy didn't understand, she added. "PSPO stuff, public order. They're bad news. Come on, let's go."

The girls broke into a run, racing across the grass, making straight for Hailey's bench.

The four Public Safety Enforcement Officers had stopped in front of Hailey and Little John. One of them, the largest of the lot, said something and pointed in the direction of Ditchling Road. Although Amy and Frances were still too far away to hear what was being said, the Enforcement Officer's authoritarian body language was unmistakable. He was telling Hailey and Little John to move on.

Hailey shook her head defiantly.

The girls were within earshot now, close enough to hear the big Enforcement Officer speak. "...no choice...I want you two out of this park..."

"I'm not going anywhere," Hailey said.

Her face was set in that hard mask of hers, but Hailey's eyes were red-rimmed and puffed up.

She's been crying. She knows. She knows about Gaz.

"Go where?" Little John asked.

"Doesn't matter, Little John," Hailey answered. "We're not going, they can't make us."

"We'll see about that." The big Enforcement Officer said gruffly. He was broad, with small mean eyes, and cheeks which had settled into heavy jowls by his chin.

The girls came to a halt by the side of the bench. The Enforcement Officer ignored them, turning to his colleagues instead. "Obvious intoxication," he said.

The others nodded, the woman adding smugly: "Unmistakable anti-social behaviour."

"I'm bloody sober!" Hailey exclaimed. "You're just making this shit up now, you idiots!"

Little John nodded solemnly, and echoed: "Idiots."

"Both turning abusive now," the female officer said.

"Hailey," Frances said. "What's going on?"

Hailey turned her head sideways, and smiled sadly when she recognised Amy and Frances. "Hullo girls. I suppose you've heard."

Amy and Frances nodded.

"You, girls," The big Enforcement Officer scowled. "Scoot. Go away. Off with you. You've got no business here."

"It's a public park," Frances said. "We have as much right to be here as you."

"Hear, hear," Hailey muttered.

The female officer studied Amy and Frances's school uniforms meaningfully. "Are you sure you're allowed to be here? At this time of day?"

Frances ignored her, and asked her question again. "What's going on here?"

"None of your damn business," one of the other Enforcement Officers growled. "Now you heard the man, be off with you."

Frances shook her head defiantly. "I'm staying right here."

"So am I," Amy declared bravely.

The big officer shrugged. "All the same to me, you're not going to be able to help these two."

153

"We've done nothing wrong!" Hailey protested.

"There is a Public Spaces Protection Order in effect for The Level," the big officer told her. "And through your anti-social behaviour, you are in breach of the PSPO."

"Anti-social behaviour?" Hailey shook her head. "We're just sitting there, minding our own business. That's not in breach of anything."

"You have been abusive towards us," the female officer said, with satisfaction in her voice. "We all heard it."

"Sufficient to warrant a Fixed Penalty Notice," the big officer added. "So you're going to have to cough up one hundred pounds, if you want to keep this out of court."

"A hundred quid?!" Frances exclaimed. "Where are homeless people supposed to get a hundred quid from?"

"If they refuse to pay," the female officer said, "which is their right, then they can argue their case in front of a magistrate."

"Yeah right," Hailey said. "Our word against yours."

"Precisely," the big officer declared. "You haven't got a chance in hell, Sunshine, and then the magistrate will fine you a thousand pounds. It's up to you, a hundred pound FPN now, or a thousand pounds later."

"This is ridiculous!" Frances exclaimed.

Amy looked at the officers in disbelief.

They're just bullies. More trolls.

"It's the law," the big officer insisted. "But I'll tell you what. Get up and leave the park, like I asked before, and I'll disregard the PSPO breach and forget about the FPN."

He looked at Hailey with a triumphant grin. Hailey shook her head, a bitter expression on her face.

"Hailey," Frances said. "Maybe..."

"No. I won't give them the satisfaction." Hailey crossed her arms, her expression one of sheer stubbornness. "I'm sick and tired of being pushed around like I'm a bit of inconvenient rubbish. Today of all days."

"Just leave her alone!" Amy appealed to the officers. "Her best friend died last night. He was found this morning. Can't you see she's upset?"

The female officer laughed, and asked Hailey: "Your big friend here not enough for you?"

Hailey glared at her.

"One useless drunk less." The big officer shrugged. "They'll bag and burn him. Good riddance, I say."

"No!" Frances shouted, at the same time that Hailey unleashed a torrent of expletives.

"RIGHT YOU LOT!" The big officer thundered. "I've had enough. I asked you nicely, now I'm telling you to get the hell out this park."

He stepped forward and grabbed Hailey's arm, attempting to pull her off the bench.

Everything seemed to happen at once. Hailey hissed and snarled, clutching the back of the bench with her free arm as she resisted. The big officer cursed at her. Little John, who had spent most of the time smiling vacantly, rose with a roar, towering over everybody. He made to grab the big officer, but the other two male officers intervened, grabbing his arms. The female officer was shouting for assistance into a hand-held radio. Little John shook off his two assailants, and tried to come to Hailey's assistance again, baying like a hound, but the two men scrambled up and threw themselves at him once more. Hailey shrieked in pain. She released her grip on the bench, clutching at her wrist in the officer's grip. She was dragged off and thrown onto the ground by the big officer, who kicked her in the belly. Frances screamed in fury. So did Amy, although she was unaware of it. The big officer kicked Hailey again. She grunted and gasped. He made to kick again. Amy and Frances rushed at him. They kicked his shins and tugged at his arms. He cursed them loudly.

"Meredith! Get these brats off me!"

Amy felt an arm slip around her belly, and then she was lifted off the ground by the female officer. The woman was surprisingly strong and pulled Amy away, her other arm around Frances. Amy struggled. She kicked her legs about, trying to make contact with the officer's legs, but she couldn't land a proper kick. She dug her nails into the officer's hand. The officer yelped at that, but refused to let go. Frances was struggling and yelling as well.

The big officer kicked Hailey again. Little John bellowed when he saw the pain on Hailey's face. He shrugged off the two male officers restraining him, and rushed the big officer, starting to wrestle him to the ground. The pair who had been shrugged off threw themselves onto Little John's back, trying to reach for the huge man's arms. Hailey rolled away from the scrum, clutching her belly and moaning.

"Let me go!" Amy shouted, furiously.

"Let go of me!" Frances yelled.

There must have been a patrolling police car nearby, for two PCs came running, their voices joining the din. Grunts and gasps from the scrum. Radios crackled. Sirens sounded. More police arrived. Everybody was shouting. The combatants were pulled apart, Little John subdued, and the female Enforcement Officer relieved of the two kicking and hollering eleven-year-olds in her grasp. Hailey was helped up, gasping for breath. Little John looked bewildered, and started sobbing.

"He needs a tuna sandwich!" Amy shouted at no one in particular.

The big Enforcement Officer was shouting at one of the policemen, pointing angrily at Hailey and Little John, as well as the girls.

The policeman tried to calm him down, and in between doing that, signalled his colleagues. "Take them away."

Amy was dazed, but also strangely alert, ready to resume her struggle if need be. She panicked when she saw Little John being hand-cuffed, but the two police men put in charge of the girls made no move to restrain Amy or Frances with handcuffs. Instead they encouraged the girls to walk with them to Union Road. Other PCs escorted Little John in the same direction, and they were followed by Hailey, who had trouble walking and was leaning on the supporting arm of a female PC.

Passer-bys stopped to watch, and curious faces looked at the procession from behind their car windows. Hailey and Little John were led to a van. Amy and Frances were instructed to take a seat in the back of a police car. People pointed. The doors were shut. Amy and Frances exchanged an incredulous glance, as two PCs got into the front seats, shut the doors, and then drove off.

"Where are you taking us?" Frances demanded to know.

"Brighton Police Station."

Amy filled with despair on hearing that, but then caught Frances looking at her. Her friend had opened her eyes as wide as possible, and her mouth formed a gaping round 'O', like a cartoon character in shock. Despite the whole rotten day, Amy had to laugh.

"It's no joke, Missy," one of the PC's said sternly.

Amy imitated Frances's comical look, and this time Frances laughed.

"Kids these days," the PC muttered, and the other shook his head and sighed.

23. Interrogation at John Street

When they arrived at Brighton Police Station, Amy craned her neck to try and spot Hailey and Little John. She wanted to…

I don't even know.

Get reassurance somehow? Catch a glimpse of someone familiar in a sea of strange faces? It was all so weird. Amy was still trying to make sense of what had just happened on The Level, and the large police station was a new overwhelming experience to digest.

There were police everywhere: walking, standing, sitting. Some peered intently at computer screens, others cradled a steaming mug, many were talking to each other, or into phones. Yet more carried piles of paperwork from one place to another. A number of them threw curious glances at the girls, as the two PCs guided them through a maze of corridors.

They arrived in large office, with more than a dozen workstations, flanked by a waiting room of sorts. The two rooms were separated by a row of counters.

One of the desks in the office was occupied by a female officer, with a kind, motherly face framed by half-long, jet-black hair. She rose as the girls were brought in, picking up a sheaf of forms. To Amy's surprise, she was short for an adult, only a bit taller than Amy was.

"Sarge," one of the escorting PCs said. "These are the girls from The Level."

"I'm Sergeant Roberts," the woman introduced herself to the girls. "Shall we find somewhere quiet to sit?"

Amy and Frances followed her into a small adjoining room. The room was bare, except for a table and four chairs, and a round clock mounted on one of the walls. Another door led to the waiting room.

Sergeant Roberts motioned the girls to sit down, and then arranged the forms she had been carrying into several piles. When she was done, she gave the girls a puzzled look. They were both still standing.

"Have we been arrested?" Frances asked.

"Arrested?" Sergeant Roberts smiled. "No, dear, you're in temporary custody, that's all."

"Why?" Amy asked. "What have we done wrong?"

"I'd like to go home now," Frances said.

Sergeant Roberts took a seat, and observed the girls thoughtfully for a few short moments. "Very well, I will tell you formally then, that there is such a thing as mandatory school attendance. We are assuming, at this moment, that you two are truants."

She paused, and gave a friendly smile, but her eyes were daring Amy and Frances to deny the obvious.

Amy nodded, after which Frances said: "True, but..."

"We'll get to the 'but' in a bit," Sergeant Roberts said. "We don't often haul truants into the station, but seeing that the both of you were engaged in a small battle with Public Safety Enforcement Officers..."

Her voice trailed off. Amy and Frances exchanged a worried glance.

Just how much trouble are we in?

The sergeant continued: "There is sufficient reason to be concerned about your safety, and temporary custody is a reasonable precautionary measure. Now, if you two could please sit down? The sooner we get through this...," she pointed at the forms on the table, "...the sooner you'll be on your way home."

Amy and Frances sat down. There had been so much going on, that Amy hadn't thought about her parents yet, but she now realised that the police were bound to contact them. Amy felt dizzy; it was as if she was plunging into a deep, dark hole.

Sergeant Roberts confirmed her worst fears, when she took down their names and ages first, and then asked how the girls' parents could be contacted.

One of the policemen who had brought them over from The Level popped into the room.

"PC Twyner and I have started writing our reports, Sarge," He said. "Just checking if there's anything you need doing?"

"Thank you PC Tuppen. There are a few phone calls that need to be made. Parents first, then contact the school." She picked up the first forms she had filled in, and showed it to the PC, pointing at various places.

Amy looked at Frances. Frances shrugged helplessly, then reached out under the table. Amy reached out too, clutching her friend's hand to hold it tightly.

PC Tuppen left, and the sergeant continued to take down details. Dates of birth, height, hair colour...on and on it went.

"Tattoos?" She asked.

"We're only eleven!" Frances exclaimed.

"Eleven-point-two-five, and eleven-point-five," Amy said, because she felt it was important to be accurate.

The sergeant grinned. "You'd be surprised. But alright, no tattoos I take it."

Time crawled to a near standstill, as the sergeant continued working her way through the forms. Every second indicated by the ticking clock seemed to pass by in slow-motion.

It was a strange sensation, after the manic morning which had involved the confrontation in the loos, the rush downtown, the rising anger at the sheer injustice on The Level, the struggle with the PSPO Trolls, being driven through the streets of Brighton in police custody...

160

Amy was aware it was also the calm eye of the storm, because the day was far from over yet. Even as they progressed through the forms, parents were being called. What would they do? Would they come to the police station? Would they be angry? Amy recalled the solemn promise they had made to Mr Greenwood; to think first, and act later. Would he be angry?

Her mind's eye kept on replaying the image of Hailey, curled up on the grass, helpless as she was repeatedly kicked by that big Enforcement Officer.

When Sergeant Roberts announced that it was time to take down a joint statement, the girls unleashed a torrent of words.

"They were going to stick our heads down the loos and flush."

"They would have killed us!"

"If they found us after."

"And Gaz was found dead."

"They weren't doing anything."

"They weren't drunk!"

"They were just sitting there."

"They said it was good that Gaz was going to be bagged and burned."

"He kicked her. He was kicking her. For no reason!"

"Whoa! Whoa!" The Sarge raised her hands in front of her. "One thing at a time, let's start at the beginning. School."

Amy and Frances slowed down, and relived the events at school that morning, occasionally interrupting each other to clarify details. The police woman listened patiently, made notes, and asked questions. She didn't offer argument when the girls added incensed opinions to their stories, but when Sergeant Roberts read the first part of the joint statement out loud, Amy noted that it was just the basic facts that she had written down.

The girls took their cue from this, and did their best to give a less opinionated account of events on The Level. Nevertheless, it was hard for them to avoid outrage when they reported on the taunting by the PSPO Trolls, and then the physical violence inflicted on Hailey.

"She was already down on the ground. She couldn't do anything!" Frances said.

"He started kicking her. In the tummy, like really hard," Amy added.

"That's why we rushed him." Frances explained. "I didn't even think about it...," she turned to Amy, "...did you?"

Amy shook her head. There had been no time to think, things just happened really quickly and she had reacted to them instinctively. "And then that woman Troll grabbed us..."

"Troll?" Sergeant Roberts asked.

"Enforcement Officer," Frances explained.

"I see," the Sergeant replied. "So you two did intervene with the Public Safety Enforcement Officer? He claimed that you 'assaulted' him."

"The Big Troll was kicking Hailey!" Amy protested. "She was on the gro..."

"Yes, we've established that. What precisely did you do, in this...'assault' of yours?"

"I kicked his shin," Frances declared with satisfaction. "Twice."

"We were trying to grab his arms," Amy said. "To make him stop attacking Hailey. Where is Hailey?"

"Hailey might have been hurt," Frances said. "She should see a doctor. Little John was really upset as well. People think he's dangerous because he's so big."

"But he's not," Amy added. "He just doesn't understand things quickly."

"Let me just round this off, and then I'll tell you about the other two," Sergeant Roberts said. "You said the female Public

Safety Enforcement Officer grabbed you both by the middle, and pulled you away…"

"She was strong," Amy said. "I tried to get free, but she wouldn't let go."

"It hurt," Frances said. She rubbed her neck. "I think I've got whiplash. Can I sue her? Will you arrest all of them?"

The corners of the sergeant's mouth twitched, but she kept a straight face. "Whiplash is generally not an injury associated with being grabbed by the middle, so I don't think you have much of a case there."

"Oh," Frances sounded disappointed.

"There is one more thing I want to be clear about. Did I understand correctly that you confirmed that Hailey was using abusive language?"

"It wasn't like that…" Frances shook her head.

"They were being horrible to her…" Amy said.

"Yes, or no?" The sergeant looked from girl to girl.

"Well…" Amy began.

"…Yes, but…" Frances started.

"Thank you," Sergeant Roberts said. "Give me a moment please."

She started writing on her statement form, occasionally looking at the notes she had taken. The other police man from The Level, Amy remembered that PC Tuppen had named him PC Twyner, came in with two plastic cups filled with lukewarm tea, which the girls accepted gratefully.

"You haven't got any chocolate, have you?" Frances asked jokingly. "I'll write you a great review on Trip Advisor."

PC Twyner grinned, shook his head, and left again.

"Right," Sergeant Roberts said. "You two ready?"

Just as she had for the first part of the statement about school that morning, she now read out the second part of the joint statement about events on The Level.

It was strange to listen to an account of her experiences as understood and written down by somebody else. Amy mostly recalled it as a rapid succession of extreme emotions. Sergeant Roberts's version was almost entirely devoid of emotion. Still, it was true, so Amy signed it, as did Frances.

Sergeant Roberts collected the form back from Frances, and rose to her feet. "I'll be back in a bit."

"Wait," Amy said. "You said you'd tell us where Hailey and Little John were."

"So I did. My apologies. They have been taken to hospital. The man was sedated, because nobody could calm him down, the woman because we want to make sure she hasn't sustained serious injuries."

At least they'll sleep in a dry and warm bed tonight.

Sergeant Roberts left the room to go back into the big office, closing the door behind her. Amy and Frances looked at each other. Both drew in a deep breath. It was the first time they had been alone together since crossing Ditchling Road and entering The Level.

"We're in big trouble" Frances sighed.

"Gigantic trouble," Amy agreed.

"Humongous. I'm sorry I got you into this mess."

"You got me into this mess? I was the one who said we should go find Hailey, back at school."

"Yes! No! But..."

The door to the waiting room opened, and PC Twyner stuck his head around the door. "Room service!"

They looked at him in wonder. He winked, and then he stepped into full view, holding out his hand to reveal a chocolate bar. "You'll have to share."

"Thanks! You're a life saver!" Frances took the bar, after which the policeman left again, leaving the door slightly ajar.

Amy laughed at Frances's expression. Her friend was looking at the chocolate bar as if it were made from pure gold.

Frances laughed too, then hissed: "My Preciousssssss."

They devoured the chocolate bar, after which they regretted eating it so quickly.

"I feel *sooo* much better," Frances sang out, wandering around the room with the chocolate bar wrapper in her hand, peeking into corners. "Can't see a rubbish bin."

"Stick it in a pocket."

"Hide the evidence!" Frances agreed. She stuffed the wrapper in a pocket, and paced through the room. "At least we're not in a cell."

"Not yet," Amy said darkly. "But if…"

She stopped talking when Frances halted all of a sudden.

Frances placed her index finger on her lips, and then beckoned Amy to the waiting room door, which had been left a quarter of the way open. They crept to stand at the side of the doorway, so they couldn't be seen.

There were voices in the waiting room, some of them familiar.

"I was twelve when the coppers first found reason to call me in for a chat at the local police station…"

Mr Greenwood!

"…I swear, that girl is trying to get a head start on me!"

"You may find this funny, Mr Greenwood…"

Mum!

"…but I certainly don't."

Amy's heart sank, she didn't even smile when Frances mimed her comical 'O'.

Somebody else began to speak, a man Amy didn't know.

"I'm sure, Mrs Wheatley, that Tom isn't half as amused as he's pretending to be."

"That may be, Inspector Norrell," Mum answered him, after which she appeared to be addressing Mr Greenwood. "You promised us that the girls wouldn't be left on their own with these…these homeless people. Adult supervision, that was the agreement."

"This kicked off at school," Mr Greenwood said. "I can hardly sit in on their lessons all day long, can I now? Mrs Wheatley, as far as I knew they were at school until I got the phone call from the police."

"It appears the girls were involved in a fight at school," Inspector Norrell informed them. "With three older pupils. I understand the parents of the other girls were eager to file a complaint of sorts."

"Frances did mention that there were three Year 9 girls 'out to get them'," Mr Greenwood said.

"I don't know what's come over Amy lately," Mum declared. "It's totally not in her character to pick fights at school, and then play truant. She's never skived off school before she met your Frances."

Amy took in a deep breath, and looked at Frances apologetically. Frances shrugged to show indifference, but Amy could tell that she was hurt.

"What are you suggesting, Mrs Wheatley?" Mr Greenwood asked.

"Truth be told," Inspector Norrell said. "It's not the school, nor the skiving I'm most concerned about. We've had contact with the school, they told us that the three older pupils are notorious bullies. I'm far more worried about what happened at The Level. The girls were involved in a scuffle between two homeless people and four Public Safety Enforcement Officers."

"Involved in what?" Mum asked, shocked.

"Another fight?" Mr Greenwood asked. "Is Frances okay?"

"Where is Amy?" Mum asked. "I want to see her, I want to see my daughter."

"The girls are fine," Inspector Norrell said. "A little bit shaken, I'm told, but otherwise unhurt. They've been talking to us calmly, and we've taken down their statements. You'll see them soon enough."

"What precisely happened?" Mr Greenwood inquired.

The inspector said: "What I know is that my people were called out to The Level by PSPO officers."

"The PSPO," Mum said thoughtfully.

"Public Spaces Protection Order," Mr Greenwood said.

"I'm aware of that, Mr Greenwood," Mum pointed out. "I work at a law firm."

"Nice on paper, but in practice..." Mr Greenwood continued unperturbed. "First they cut police funding, then they outsource tasks the police can't carry out anymore. The contracts get picked up by private companies. They stick badly-trained thugs in uniforms, and send them onto the streets, after which they send sky-high bills at the tax payer's expense."

"I'm not at liberty to describe it like that," the Inspector said. "But Tom said it well enough."

"What does that have to do with Amy?" Mum asked.

"The Enforcement Officers called for police assistance," Inspector Norrell answered. "They stated that they were attempting to carry out their authorised duties, dealing with a breach of the public order by a homeless man and woman. That the girls appeared and supposedly physically assaulted one of the officers."

"Have you seen the size of them?" Mr Greenwood asked incredulously. "They're just wee sprites, the both of them."

"What breach of public order?" Mum asked. "Were they addicts?"

Amy couldn't see Mum, from her concealment by the doorway, but she was pretty sure Mum gave Mr Greenwood a pointed look, when she asked that last question.

Inspector Norrell sighed loud enough for Amy to hear. "The Enforcement Officers said the two homeless people were exhibiting anti-social behaviour. If that is true, it lies within their remit to…"

"What behaviour?" Mum persisted.

"They said, that although no bottles were found, the two appeared intoxicated, and were hurling abuse at passer-by's."

"Shouting drunks." Mum snorted. "And you, Mr Greenwood, think this is suitable company for a young girl to keep?"

"I think that the Inspector has only told us the PSPO version of events so far," Mr Greenwood answered. "And I already have reasons to doubt it. Frances may be impulsive, but she isn't daft, far from it. She knows well enough never to go anywhere near people from the street community when they appear to be using alcohol, or anything else. That's been hammered into her."

"I don't find that very reassuring," Mum said.

A door opened and shut, accompanied by footsteps.

"Ah, Sergeant Roberts," Inspector Norrell said. "Come to enlighten us?"

"I've been in touch with PC Tully, at the Royal Sussex, he's taken a statement from the woman. He's scanned the statement and mailed it over."

"How does it compare to what the girls said?" Inspector Norrell asked, before adding: "We're 100% sure that the girls didn't have a chance to speak with the others, after my people put an end to the scuffle."

"Well, Inspector," Sergeant Roberts said. "It's good we know that, because the resemblance between the woman's statement and that of the girls is uncanny."

Frances punched a fist into the air next to Amy.

"Good," Mr Greenwood said. "So what's the other side of the story?"

"Sergeant Roberts?" Inspector Norrell asked.

"The pair in the park were sitting there, sober, when the PSPO officers showed up. They demanded that the two homeless people move out of the park, and threatened them with a Fixed Penalty Notice. It appears that the woman was then goaded into giving a hostile verbal reaction. The team leader of the Public Safety Enforcement Officers resorted to the physical removal of the woman. He got her down to the ground, and kicked her several times. The girls tried to stop him. They were physically restrained by one of the other Enforcement Officers."

"And," Inspector Norrell said. "Some of this can be confirmed by the first police on the scene, they witnessed the woman being kicked."

"I told you," Mr Greenwood said. "Thugs. Nothing more than thugs."

Trolls.

"But why did the girls go to The Level in the first place?" Mum wanted to know.

"Well I know what is likely to have triggered them," Mr Greenwood said.

Gaz.

"They made mention of the homeless man who was found dead in the Preston Park this morning," Sergeant Roberts said.

"Gaz. Gary Slater," Mr Greenwood said. "He is the man your daughter saved on North Street, Mrs Wheatley."

"I thought he was still in hospital," Mum replied. "Surely they don't send homeless people back on the street if they are ill?"

There was a moment of silence.

"They have been known to do that," Inspector Norrell said.

"All the time," Mr Greenwood added.

"Well," Mum said, and Amy thought she heard doubt creep into her mother's voice. "That's just...they should be helped...this is just..."

"Inhumane," Mr Greenwood said. "As a matter of fact, two years ago, a programme was put in place to ensure that homeless people were provided with a short transition period after a hospital stay, in a B&B, hotel, or emergency accommodation."

"Was this Mr Slater not eligible?" Mum asked.

"I don't know," Mr Greenwood answered. "The programme was outsourced to a small private company. They've been receiving over 25 grand a year funding, but nobody in the street community, or outreach teams for that matter, has ever seen or talked to anybody from that company. Nor has a single homeless person been offered a transition place after a hospital stay."

"That's outrageous," Mum admitted. "And somebody should do something about that, but not my daughter. Trained professionals have trouble engaging with members of this 'street community' of yours. It's simply not responsible to let eleven-year-olds anywhere near these people. You seem to imply, Mr Greenwood, that all of them are saints, but you know as well as I do, that a lot of them are up to no good, conning the public for money, shooting up dope in public places for all to see, leaving their filthy needles strewn about in parks, twittens, shop doorways."

"I know that there are a few hard-core users, and they're not making it any easier for the rest, if only because they re-enforce public stereotypes," Mr Greenwood countered. "We've got a lot of people with mental health issues out there, who are not receiving anything useful in terms of care or treatment. A lot of ex-armed servicemen and women as well, sent to Afghanistan or Iraq, come back haunted and the dumped back into civvy life completely unprepared. I also know that a lot of the money allocated to help these people is seen as easy profits by some, or supplemental income for local authority budgets. Nobody seems to care."

"Still," Mum persisted. "Eleven-year-olds..."

"That is something we both agree on," Mr Greenwood said. "I can use the helping hands at the Street Kitchen, which is a controlled situation. I don't approve of the girls going off on missions of their own devising. Both Frances and Amy know this. I've had a frank chat with them about it, and was under the impression that they had made certain promises to me..."

Amy and Frances exchanged a guilty look at this.

"Meaning your trust in them has been misplaced," Mum said, with the satisfaction of having scored a goal.

Amy cringed.

"It appears so," Mr Greenwood said, "but..."

"Forgive me for interrupting," Sergeant Roberts said. "But I took the girl's statement, and as I understand it, their supposed 'assault' was purely an instinctive reaction. Not surprising, I think, considering the unprofessional behaviour by the Enforcement Officers."

Amy was astonished by that, it was the first time Sergeant Roberts had given any indication as to her own opinion about what happened on The Level.

"Now, now, Sergeant." Inspector Norrell tut-tutted. "We agreed to call it 'overzealous' behaviour."

"Sorry, Inspector," Sergeant Roberts said dutifully, but Amy was convinced she didn't mean a word of it.

"Thugs, common thugs," Mr Greenwood practically spat out his opinion.

Trolls!

"What is going to happen now?" Mum asked.

Inspector Norrell replied: "As for the truancy, we will have to report it to the Council's education welfare officer. But before we do, a few of my people will interview those three older pupils from the school, at their parents' own request. They will also talk to school, for a formal statement as to the known behaviour of these three pupils."

"Good!" Mr Greenwood said. "Nothing but thugs-in-training."

More trolls.

"In our report," Inspector Norrell continued. "We will specify that the motive for the truancy was bullying. You may get a phone call, or an e-mail or two, but coming from us, the bullying will be seen as a legitimate cause. It clears you of any consequences, no fines, and no supervision or attendance orders to worry about, provided there is no repetition of this behaviour."

Amy and Frances nudged each other, both girls grinning.

"Well, that's a relief," Mum commented.

"And the business at The Level?" Mr Greenwood asked.

"Ah!" Inspector Norrell exclaimed. "That's what I am here for, Tom. To mediate between you and the Public Safety Enforcement Officers. I'm not really good at much else, am I Sergeant Roberts?"

"Not really, Inspector."

"Now the team leader of these 'overzealous' officers..."

"Thugs."

Trolls.

"...was of a mind to press charges against your daughters, to pursue the matter in court."

Amy threw her hand against her mouth to muffle her gasp.

"He was particularly taken," Inspector Norrell said. "By the notion that any sort of conviction would haunt the girls for the rest of their lives. 'That'll teach 'em to mess with me,' were his precise words."

The inspector had said that cheerfully, as if it was a good joke, but Amy suspected he wasn't at all pleased with the big Troll.

"I take back the 'thugs'," Mr Greenwood said. "These are 'goons', Bill. Do they think they're starring in their own mobster movie?"

"It's likely," Inspector Norrell said. "Which has advantages as well. I told him that if he was to press charges, I would do everything in my considerable power to ensure that the entire law-enforcement community in the whole of Sussex knew that he had been beaten up by two eleven-year-old girls."

Mr Greenwood laughed.

"You blackmailed him?" Mum asked.

"We call it persuasive negotiation," Sergeant Roberts said. "Believe me, you don't want to become embroiled in a long court procedure over this, Mrs Wheatley. It only benefits the solicitors and their fees."

"I work for a law firm, Sergeant Roberts," Mum admonished her.

"I stand by my words," the sergeant answered.

"It worked," Inspector Norrell said. "He has backed down considerably."

"But not entirely?" Mr Greenwood asked.

"That depends on you," the inspector answered. "He's not going to fully commit to this, if he thinks either you or Amy Wheatley's parents might press charges against his team."

"And you are here to practise 'persuasive negotiation' on us?" Mum asked.

"No, I thought plain and frank talk would suffice on this end," the inspector answered. "There's ground for a case, in that the Enforcement Officers should not have man-handled your children.

Their argument, however, will be that the girls initiated the physical contact, something which the girls have admitted to. So, ground for a case, but no guarantee that you'll win. I'll happily admit that I stand to gain personally from a mutual agreement to let matters rest. A court case either way would mean allocation of police time and resources, of which we have precious little. As it is, I'm extremely displeased with the behaviour of the Enforcement Officers, and the young homeless woman has a very strong case against them, with police witnesses. If you want justice, I'd recommend that you support her in any actions she might take."

"I will definitely do that, and I suspect that the Brighton and Hove Housing Coalition will offer their support as well. Other than that, I am willing to assume that everyone involved has learned a lesson from this," Mr Greenwood said. "Also because I don't want to burden Frances with court proceedings. But Bill, if they ever go after me, I'll pursue them to the gates of hell. I don't mind speaking my mind in front of a judge. And they had better not lay another finger on Frances, ever again."

"I am..." Mum hesitated. "We won't press charges."

"Good, good. Excellent." Inspector Norrell sounded relieved. "Well then, I've got to rush, I'll ask Sergeant Roberts here to re-unite you with..."

"Quick!" Frances hissed.

"...your daughters," the Inspector finished.

The girls scrambled back to their seats.

He said his goodbyes, and then they heard Sergeant Roberts say: "This way."

The door was pushed open, and Sergeant Roberts entered the room, followed by Mum and Mr Greenwood.

Upon seeing Mum, Amy had the same heart-sinking feeling she felt when she had first heard her mother's voice in the waiting room.

For a fraction of a second, Amy harboured the secret hope that Mum would sob with relief and gather Amy in her arms for a hug. Amy felt she needed a big hug, but one look at Mum's face was enough to dispel that hope.

"I am deeply ashamed of you, Amy," Mum said. "Ashamed that I've had to come to the police station to...to..." She stopped talking, and shook her head.

Amy said nothing. It struck her that Mum didn't look ashamed at all; her entire face conveyed that disapproval which clawed itself straight into Amy's heart. She tried to be a good daughter, but sometimes it seemed that trying wasn't enough for Mum, who seemed to be content with nothing else but perfection.

"Mum, you weren't there." Amy said.

"And you weren't supposed to be there." Mum bit back. "You were supposed to be at school."

Mum cast a stern look at Frances. "And I am sure your father is ashamed of you."

Frances didn't reply, looking intently at her father instead.

"I am...," Mr Greenwood paused as he searched for a word. "Defeated. I am defeated, by my trust in you. Both of you."

Amy and Frances shifted uncomfortably.

"But ashamed?" Mr Greenwood shook his head. "You did what you thought was the right thing to do. You followed your heart, Frances. I can't be ashamed of that. Mighty disappointed though, that you didn't let your mind do some of the work."

Frances nodded solemnly, then blurted out. "Dad, the Enforcement Officers, said that Gaz was going to be bagged and burned."

"Bagged and burned?" Mum asked.

"If no next-of-kin is found," Sergeant Roberts said. "Or are willing to acknowledge the deceased, then the body becomes property of the state."

"They stick them in a body bag," Mr Greenwood said. "And incinerate it. No ceremony, no words, no goodbyes."

Amy could barely believe it. She thought of Gran's funeral, all the people who had come to pay their last respects, share stories and mostly share, for a moment, the burden of grief.

"Sergeant Roberts," Mr Greenwood continued. "Could you ask Bill, Inspector Norrell, to do all he can to find the next-of-kin?"

"Are you going to organise a proper funeral, Mr Greenwood?" Amy asked.

Mr Greenwood sighed. He seemed deflated for a moment, robbed of his drive and energy. "We've had too many anonymously disposed of. Without a chance to say goodbye. I think Gaz deserves better, I truly do." He turned to the sergeant. "Gary has...had many friends on the streets. He helped out everybody when he could. Some think of him as family. I'd really appreciate it if he could have a proper send-off."

The sergeant nodded. "We'll do our best."

Frances turned to Amy, her face animated as her mind was no doubt racing with plans. "We could..."

"I don't think so," Mum cut her short. "Amy is going to be grounded for the foreseeable future."

Amy felt her world shrink already.

"They could be grounded at The Office in the afternoons," Mr Greenwood suggested. "That way these juvenile delinquents could work off their debts to society."

The surge of hope Amy felt at that proposal was immediately extinguished by Mum.

"Speaking quite frankly, Mr Greenwood," Mum said coldly. "I'm not sure that I can trust you with the safety of my child."

"Mum!" Amy protested. She dared a peek at Mr Greenwood's face, and felt horrible when she read the pain on it.

"I am sorry that you feel that way, Mrs Wheatley," he said tonelessly.

"But Mum!"

"No 'buts', Amy," Mum said. "We've tried to understand. Trusted you. Trusted him. And look where that's got us. You are grounded, and you're not to see Frances outside of school again. That's my final say on the matter."

Amy plunged into that pit of despair again, and threw a desperate look at Frances. Her friend looked back with a hopeless expression; there was nothing they could do.

24. Floating over Regency Square

The days that followed were mostly horrible. Amy's parents treated the grounding seriously. On Wednesday, after the last bell, Amy's father was waiting outside school to whisk her off home. Similarly, Mr Greenwood was waiting for Frances. When the girls got to the vehicles, Dad was standing by the open driver's window of Mr Greenwood's van, the two men in deep conversation.

Frances was taken to The Office to do sorting and homework. Amy was brought home. Dad visited Amy's room every hour or so, usually attempting good natured small talk, which she met with sullen silence. No matter how light-hearted Dad tried to make his chit-chat, Amy knew that the reason he dropped by was because Mum had told him to check on her. Although Amy had yearned for the attention before, she had hoped for it to be spontaneous, like his visits had been before Gran's passing and then Jacob's arrival. Now it felt too much of a make-believe thing, which certainly didn't fool an eleven-point-five-year-old.

Amy yearned for the freedom of roaming about North Laine, the Lanes, or the Seafront with Frances. She missed the good-natured jesting and laughter at The Office.

If Mum's intention was to cut contact between Amy and Frances as punishment, she failed miserably. Face-to-face time was cruelly short —stolen moments during the school day— but the girls resorted to digital communication. Switching effortlessly between several digital media platforms, they talked more than ever, mostly about how unfair it was that they weren't allowed to see each other.

It was also how Amy was kept informed as to Gaz's funeral plans. That evening Frances texted:

>*Insp. Norrell called Dad. They found some family<*

Amy replied.

>*YEET! Hailey+Little John?*<

Amy felt a moment of fright when she read Frances's response.

>*discharged from hospital*<

That's what happened to Gaz.

Frances allayed that fear with her next text though.

>*SWEP open. H+LJ have place 2 sleep next few nights*<

There was a moment of sweet delight at school on Thursday. Amy and Frances had just found each other in a hallway at the start of lunch break, when a classroom door opened. Two uniformed police officers came walking out, none other than PC Twyner and PC Tuppen from The Level. They were followed by the three Trolls, and some adults, all looking sheepish.

The sight of uniformed police drew curious glances from all around, and caused a buzz of excited speculation. Word soon spread that the adults were the Trolls' parents, who had involved the police because they claimed their daughters had been viciously assaulted by bullies. They were worried for the safety of their innocent, darling lambs. School had countered with a list of misdemeanours, questioning the 'innocence' of the Trolls. In the retelling of the tale, it was simplified to 'Amy and Frances from Year Seven beat up three Year Nine girls'. By the end of the day, the Trolls were followed around school by grins and sniggers, and Amy's popular classmates treated her warily, even respectfully.

After the bell rang, the girls found their respective fathers by the open back of the battered old van. Both men were drinking a cup of tea which Mr Greenwood had prepared using the Street Kitchen stuff stored in the van.

There was good news later on Thursday when Frances texted Amy:

>*Family member gave permission! Won't be there, won't pay, but gave permission!!*<

That same evening, Mr Greenwood launched an online crowd-funding campaign. The description of the crowdfunder was a heartfelt plea to help the street community pay their last respects to Gaz with some human dignity. Amy cried a little when she read the words.

The girls checked the progress of the crowdfunder hourly, messaging each other to report each increase. It was mostly fivers or tenners, from people who left behind comments that they had little to spare but wanted to contribute. Every now and then, Amy and Frances would exchange a string of smiley icons when exceptionally generous amounts came in. Some people donated fifty pounds, a hundred even. An anonymous donation came in for two hundred pounds, and the girls opened a video chat to sing 'We are the Champions' in celebration.

On Friday afternoon, the fathers were drinking tea again by the back of the open van, this time also nibbling on a pack of biscuits which Amy's dad had brought along. The men joked about having a fully loaded picnic table by the end of the next week, or maybe a winter barbeque. Neither Amy nor Frances were much amused.

On Friday evening Frances texted:

>*It's happening. Dad got agreement Bear Rd*<

The crowdfunding campaign reached, and then bypassed, its target on Saturday evening. Mr Greenwood had done it. The digital chatter between Amy and Frances reached new heights as they discussed it non-stop. Frances had more news as well:

>*Hailey helping organise. Even going 2B a vicar. Next Wed afternoon. Proper funeral. Pls come if u can*<

Amy was incredibly pleased with all the news, though it was mixed with sadness. She had asked her parents if she could go, and Mum had replied with a resounding 'No!'

The rest of the weekend was a nightmare. Amy was stuck in her room both days, unwilling to venture into the house unless she absolutely had to. Both her parents were pretending things were as normal. They avoided talk of The Level and the grounding, but it made all other subject matters seem fake.

After the weekend, the Monday and Tuesday were as the end of the previous week had been, with both Dad and Mr Greenwood waiting outside of school after the bell. On Tuesday, though, Dad didn't take the route home after picking Amy up, heading downtown instead.

"Where are we going?" Amy asked.

"I thought I'd take you on a surprise outing," Dad said cheerfully. "You used to like those, I recall."

"I'm grounded! Remember?"

"I am well aware. But you've worn me down with all your moping. I can't bear to see you so miserable. I thought, maybe, we could conjure up a smile. Just a little one, before I forget what they look like."

Amy put on her fakest smile, with as little conviction as she could manage.

"I see…" Dad said, disappointment in his voice.

"You can't ground me to prevent me from seeing Frances, and then think it's fair to un-ground me when it suits you. Or can I see Frances after?"

"Your mum and I are worried about the influence…"

"Dad, the North Street thing would have happened with, or without Frances. She wasn't with me, I told you I was walking to the bus stop from Churchill Square, on my own."

"It was The Level we were thinking of."

They were on Richmond Place, passing St Peter's, and Amy noticed two patrolling Public Safety Enforcement Officers. She glared at them, hating them with her eyes.

"Frances didn't want to go downtown after the fight at school." Amy said. "I made her come with me. I'm the bad influence."

She stared out of the window, feeling even more miserable than before, because she knew she was being horrid to her father. More than he deserved, anyway. There was just so much bottled-up frustration!

Dad stayed silent. Amy could sense his disappointment. Although Amy wanted to say something nice to make things better, she couldn't bring herself to do so, so stared out of the window instead, as the car made its way through the busy streets of central Brighton.

It turned out that Dad had booked tickets for the i360, the incredibly tall metal funnel by the old West Pier, with the steel and glass donut-shaped pod which was always slowly travelling up and down the towering mast.

Secretly, Amy was thrilled. Like most Brightonians, she hadn't been sure what to make of the i360 at first. It caught the eye because it could be seen from all over town, but that was its height rather than the merits of its design. Amy also resented the fact that the big wheel near the Palace Pier, which she had always loved, had been removed, apparently in exchange for the i360. As the months had passed, however, the towering construction had become a familiar sight, and when it was dark the pod was spectacular to behold, it's steel and glass all lit up like a visiting flying saucer.

Rising slowly into the sky in the pod was mesmerising. Amy had always wondered what Brighton looked like to the many seagulls lazily riding the sky above the city, and now she discovered what she had suspected. Brighton was simply beautiful from this vantage point. She was also delighted to see that they even surpassed the seagulls in altitude, for she was looking down on their backs as they glided over the rooftops.

"It takes all the imperfections away, like this, doesn't it?" Dad marvelled. "All the graffiti, overflowing bins, and crumbling buildings."

Amy thought of the small park outside of St Barts. If you looked in the direction of London Road, your eyes would meet the unkempt rear ends of the shops fronting London Road. There were rows of wheelie bins parked below the BORN AND BRED sign, attracting unwanted attention from seagulls. Every available surface was covered in graffiti. Some ugly, but Amy liked most of it, and there was funny stuff as well. To her, that was Brighton too, just as much as the Pavilion or the Palace Pier.

They circled the pod, pausing to take in the skeletal remains of the West Pier. Amy knew the story well enough. Once upon a time it had been the best pier in Brighton, more beautiful even than the Palace Pier. After it shut, people talked for years about saving the West Pier, but nobody did. Neglect was followed by disrepair. Battered by storms, sections had begun to collapse. Then there had been the great fire, which had consumed most of the pier. This had been several years before Amy was born, but people still talked about it, always in terms of personal grief, and the trauma of losing the Queen of Brighton had rubbed off on her.

Watching the rusting piles rising from the waves from a bird's-eye view gave Amy a whole new perspective of the West Pier, the layout a poignant reminder of past glories.

A Ghost.

They circled back to the town-side of the pod again. The sea of rooftops rising up and down like waves, the great expanse of the South Downs beyond the city limits, familiar landmarks...Brighton.

It was funny how being able to see the whole city at once was accompanied by a feeling of detachment. High up above the rooftops of even the grand hotels along the seafront, the city felt distant, as if Amy wasn't a part of it anymore but had become a spectator. It was how she had experienced the last week really, like a bystander on the sidelines.

"I was hoping you'd enjoy it," Dad said. "Perhaps I should have asked first, if this is something you..."

"Dad. It's beautiful. Really beautiful. I'm enjoying it. "

"Ah, I wasn't sure...you don't seem very happy."

Amy sighed. "Dad, you want me to be honest. And now you want me to be happy. Right now, I can't be honest if I pretend to be happy."

"Fair enough," Dad agreed.

"Dad, it's not fair that I can't see Frances. She's my friend. All we did was stand up to bullies."

"It wasn't quite..."

"Yes it was Dad. They were adults, but adults can be bullies too. And we were standing up to them. Remember what you and Mum told me? 'Always stand up to bullies'. That's what I did."

"It's actually more complicated than that."

"No. You always try to say things are really complicated and I'm not old enough to understand...but this wasn't complicated. They were kicking someone for no reason. They are bullies."

"It is more complicated, because there are...," Dad paused for a moment, a thoughtful look on his face. "There are things you don't know about, which we haven't told you because...yes...well...we were waiting until you were older."

"Dad, I'm eleven..."

"...point-five. I know you are. Listen, I can understand it if you think your mother's reaction has been...strange."

"It has been! I know I deserve some punishment because we didn't keep our promise, but...you don't know what it was like at school! What if Frances finds another friend? Someone who can come to The Office and help out at the Clock Tower? And why can't I go the funeral? It's the last time..."

"Your mother has good reasons, very good reasons, to be distrustful of people living out on the streets, Amy. You must believe me."

"Then tell me! Please. I'm old enough to know that bad things happen."

Dad nodded. "I think the time has come, yes. But I'll need to talk to your mum first, and she should be the one to tell you.

It was all very intriguing and Amy's curiosity was aroused, but Dad's request seemed reasonable, so she nodded her agreement.

"I understand that Tom Greenwood managed to raise enough money, with his crowdfunding campaign," Dad said.

"He's lit," Amy said full of conviction. "And all the people who donated."

"It's very generous of them," Dad agreed. "And Tom is a very interesting man to talk to."

"You've talked to him all week." Amy realised. "Has he talked about homeless stuff?"

"He appears to know a lot about it. I must admit, that I was…"

"…wrong." Amy suggested.

Dad frowned briefly, then nodded. "Yes, I was wrong." He cleared his throat. "I'm supposed to find out if you've had time to reflect, you know, contemplate your sins and things…"

"I have had time to think," Amy said.

"Oh, good!" Dad sounded relieved.

"And I wouldn't do anything differently," Amy declared. "I'm glad I stood up for my friends. My parents taught me to always stand up to bullies."

She could see that it wasn't the reaction her Dad had hoped for, but the corner of his mouth twitched, as if her were about to smile.

"I'm just being honest, Dad," Amy reminded him.

"So you are," he replied. "Very well then, I'll report that back to your mum. And I'll also talk to her about the funeral."

"YOU WILL?"

"If I were you," he said. "I would want to go."

"Oh, thank you Dad!"

Amy leaned against him, and he folded an arm around her shoulder. They stood like that for the entire descent, back to the ground, back to Brighton.

25. A Goodbye on Bear Road

Big John and Tamara were outside a chapel, when Amy and her father got to the crematorium which was surrounded by a serene sloped cemetery. Big John was holding a big bin bag, and Tamara had label stickers and markers in her hand. Her head was turned towards a man who was just walking inside.

"Don't worry Ed, it's labelled, and you'll get it back afterwards. Promise." She turned, already talking again. "Right you lot, any booze, I'm confiscating it...oh, hi Amy!"

Amy introduced Dad to Tamara and Big John. Dad offered his condolences, then said: "I didn't bring any...wasn't aware it'd be like an Irish wake."

"Some of them..." Tamara sighed, then looked at Dad apologetically. "You mustn't think the worst of them, when you haven't got a place to live, it's hard to know what to do with your stuff, so they carry it all with them. Tom asked us to collect tins and bottles for the duration."

"Wake's on The Level, tonight," Big John said. "They'll have them back again by then."

"What time?" Amy asked.

"Amy, that's a 'no'," Dad said sternly.

"Pushing her luck, is she?" Tamara asked, grinning at Amy's disappointed expression.

"You have no idea." Dad sighed.

"Oh but I do, mine's fourteen." Tamara sighed far deeper.

"The awkward age," Dad commiserated.

Amy rolled her eyes.

"It's fun inside," Tamara said with a wide grin, indicating the door. "The funeral director is having a nervous breakdown."

"Oh dear," Dad said.

"She hasn't bargained on Tom Greenwood doing things his own way," Big John said.

"Or Frances Greenwood." Tamara added with relish.

"Tom was still messing about in the van," Big John continued. "So wee Frances arrived before he did, to find a bunch of rough sleepers being told to stay outside by the funeral director."

"The mourners must stay outside," Tamara said, imitating a high posh voice, "until the body arrives and the coffin's brought in."

"Well, our Frances weren't having it, was she now?" Big John chuckled. "She gave the director an earful that would have left a drill instructor blushing. Made abundantly clear that it's rude to keep homeless people waiting out in the winter cold which caused the death of one of them."

Amy laughed, able to picture the entire scene.

"The director probably thought that was the worst of it," Big John continued. "But then she got Tom on her plate."

"It's not customary," Tamara mimicked in the falsetto voice, "to have tea or coffee before the ceremony."

"So she's been double Greenwooded," Big John concluded with satisfaction. "The doors are open for all, and there's a hot cup of tea or coffee for people to wrap their cold hands around."

"Tom warned me that this would be unlike any other funeral," Dad said. "I've never been to a homeless funeral before, to be honest."

"No one has!" Tamara exclaimed. "Or at least, not that I know of. This is pretty special."

"We did carry those six empty coffins about on Brighton streets a few years back, remember?" Big John asked Tamara. "In the 'no more deaths on our streets' protest."

"Yeah." Tamara grinned. "That sure gave passer-by's something to think about, still, it's not the same."

Amy and Dad went into the chapel. Amy bit on her lip, when she saw the table draped by a large cloth at the front. That's where they would put the coffin. Gaz's coffin.

Looking away, she recognised the set-up in the improvised tea and coffee corner. Clare was there, pouring hot drinks, just as if they had been at the Clock Tower. She was using the folding table, big water cans and all the tins with coffee, tea, and sugar which they used for the street kitchen.

The chapel had already filled up. Most of the people were standing around, talking. A few had taken seats. Amy recognised a lot of them. She saw Little John, as well as Frank, Sue, and Kirsty from The Office. The elderly man who had directed the girls to The Level on the day that Gaz had been found...

He's called Jimmy.

...was talking to Mr Greenwood and a vicar.

Where is Frances? And Hailey?

"A lot of people," Dad said. "And they paid for this with that crowdfunding campaign?"

"Yes."

"Impressive. But I would've thought that...I expected..."

"What, Dad?"

"Well, more homeless people." Dad shifted about uncomfortably. "It's nice that all these people have come, of course...but I thought it was also to give the people on the streets a chance to..."

"Dad!" Amy stifled a laugh.

"What? Did I..."

Amy smiled. Frances had kept her digitally updated. They had been hard at work at The Office. A lot of people had been given a chance to shower, shave, polish, and shine. Whole bin bags of previously unsuitable donations had revealed a treasure trove of formal clothing, useless out on the streets, but suitable for a funeral. About a third of the people they saw were simply dressed in their daily street gear, but the rest had benefitted from an Office makeover. Upon a closer look, it became apparent that many of the clothes Gaz's friends were wearing were mismatched. Little John especially, stood out, wearing a blazer that was threatening to burst at the seams, and trousers which reached no lower than his calves, leaving socks to cover the lower part of his legs.

"I didn't mean to be disrespectful," Dad said, regarding Amy's smile with a puzzled look on his face.

"Dad, almost everyone here is homeless…"

"What?" Dad looked around in surprise. "They seem so…they're…"

"Almost human," Amy supplied.

Dad looked embarrassed.

"It's okay," Amy assured him. "I was surprised when we visited Gaz in hospital and Hailey was all dressed up…"

"Josh! Amy!" Mr Greenwood had spotted them and came striding over. Amy was shocked by how tired he looked.

"Tom." Dad offered a hand.

Mr Greenwood grasped Dad's hand in both of his. "I can't thank you enough for bringing Amy."

Dad nodded. "It was good of you to arrange this."

"You wouldn't believe how much work it took," Mr Greenwood rumbled. "It's remarkable that local authorities who were happy to ignore and neglect Gaz when he was alive, were suddenly very concerned about his well-being after he died. They appeared to be worried that I was a Victorian body-snatcher, eager to sell Gaz's body to dodgy scientists to make a quick bob or two. Anyhow, your donation to the crowdfunder was much appreciated, Josh."

"You donated?" Amy asked her father in surprise.

"A little," Dad mumbled.

"A bit more than that." Mr Greenwood beamed.

"Oh Dad! Thank you!"

Dad looked at his feet, then turned his face to Amy. "Should I be honest?" He asked with a wink.

Amy nodded gravely. "Always."

"It was purely selfish," Dad confessed. "I was hoping to compensate a bit, for not paying you enough attention. Buying off one sin with another, I suppose." He pulled a long face.

Amy forgave him readily, pleased that he had helped out. She was struck by the thought that he must have donated long before their flight on the i360, when things back home had still been tense.

"Well, if it's sins you need absolution from, Josh," Mr Greenwood said. "Here's the man to talk to."

Amy looked to see the vicar approach them. For a moment she was puzzled, trying to work out his age. There was something grandfatherly about him, with short cropped white hair on the sides of his otherwise bare head, and the old-fashioned broad, black upper frames of his glasses. On the other hand, he had a quick, light step, and when he smiled at Mr Greenwood his face conveyed youthful energy. To Amy's surprise, that smile faded when the vicar looked at Dad, to be replaced by a puzzled look.

Dad gasped. "Vincent?"

"Josh!" The vicar smiled again, and seized Dad's hand to shake it with vigour. "I thought you looked familiar."

"Fancy meeting you here in Brighton, after London...how many years ago?"

"Oh, more than I care to remember," the vicar said. "I hope Nancy is well?"

"Yes, she's doing well."

"I am very pleased to hear that. And who is this?" The vicar smiled at Amy. "She reminds me of Nancy."

"My manners!" Dad exclaimed. "This is our daughter Amy. Amy, this is Reverend Cooper."

"Hello," Amy said. "Pleased to meet you."

"I have heard a lot about you, Amy. Frances told me you are a remarkable friend."

Frances!

"Do you know where she is?" Amy asked hopefully.

"That I do," Reverend Cooper said, pointing towards the front of the chapel. "She's taken a seat already."

Amy looked at Dad, to see if it was okay to join Frances, but he had started an earnest conversation with Mr Greenwood, so she slipped away and made her way to the front of the chapel.

Like the vicar had said, Frances and Hailey had taken seats on the front row already. Frances jumped up, and the girls embraced, holding on to each other tightly.

"I'm glad you came," Frances said, when they released each other at last.

"So am I," Amy said, and then impulsively gave Hailey a hug.

"Huh" Hailey grunted, hesitated for a moment, and then hugged back. "Now don't you think I'm going soft on you, girl."

Amy stepped back, shaking her head with a small grin.

"Sit down," Hailey indicated the empty seats.

"Isn't the front row for family?" Amy asked, before remembering that Frances had texted to say that whatever family member of Gaz's had been found wouldn't be attending

"We are his family now," Hailey said with a sad smile. "He'll have to make do with us."

Amy sat down next to Hailey, and Frances returned to her seat on Hailey's other side.

Others started moving towards the seats now. Mr Greenwood came to the front followed by the vicar and Amy's father.

"Remember, Rev," Mr Greenwood said to the vicar. "This lot are a wild bunch compared to your usual crowd. A lot of mental health issues. I'll use my killer stare on those who get out of hand

and make too much noise, but don't expect them to stay quiet all the time. Not all of them are big on the Church."

"You've given me ample warning Tom," the reverend replied. "Several times this week, as a matter of fact."

"He talks too much," Frances chimed in. "I'm trying to teach him not to."

Reverend Cooper smiled. "I'll do my best, go with the flow as it were."

"Thanks again," Mr Greenwood said. "Josh?"

Mr Greenwood indicated the seat next to Amy, before he himself sat down next to Frances.

It was funny to introduce Dad to Hailey. Amy recalled the scene outside of the London Road Co-Op, when Mum had lashed out at Hailey. It had only been a few weeks ago, yet seemed so much longer. Who could have thought back then, that Dad would now be politely offering his condolences to Hailey?

Amy looked at Reverend Cooper, who was standing patiently in a corner, waiting for everybody to find a seat. Craning her neck to look behind her, Amy saw people were still coming in, enough to fill all the seats.

"Hailey," she asked. "Do you believe in God?"

Hailey shook her head. "If I did, I'd have to blame him for all the bloody misery I see every day. The whole system is rotten. But Gaz did believe."

"Really?"

There's so much I don't know about him.

"Regular church-goer," Hailey confirmed. "He attended services before, and after, the Clock Tower kitchen on Sundays. And not like some, just to keep out of the rain. That's why Tom asked the vicar to come. But if he tells us that 'God works in mysterious ways', I might just scream."

"He won't," Mr Greenwood said confidently. "He's one of the good ones. They do meals at his church, St Luke's."

Amy hid a smile, liking the fact that Mr Greenwood's estimation of people was partially measured in their efforts to help the street community.

A hush fell over the chapel, when six pall-bearers entered, with slow, purposeful steps, bearing a simple coffin on their shoulders. Amy stared at the coffin, finding it hard to believe that Gaz was actually laid out in there. It seemed so final, and she felt her eyes grow moist as she followed the progress of the pall-bearers. They carefully set the coffin down on the table, and then exited the chapel.

Reverend Cooper slowly walked to Gaz's coffin, until he was standing by its side. He laid his hand on the lid, lowered his head and closed his eyes for a moment, his lips moving in a silent prayer. The chapel hushed, and people waited, some expectantly, some with an air of resistance.

The reverend opened his eyes again, turned to face the chapel, and began to speak: "Tom Greenwood has warned me that you'll be the toughest crowd I've ever played..."

"You betcha," Hailey murmured softly.

"...isn't that how you formulated it, Tom?"

"Indeed!" Mr Greenwood confirmed, to chuckles from others in the chapel.

"He told me," the reverend continued. "That it was a once-in-a-lifetime opportunity for me to surround myself with the wildest of heathens..."

Mr Greenwood grinned.

"But then," the reverend said. "I don't suppose he knows Brighton very well, because I do that on a daily basis, every time I step outside."

He drew laughs with that one, breaking some of the tension. Hailey laughed as well.

Amy didn't have much experience in the way of funerals, but it struck her that this was an odd way to start one. It was a relief to laugh though, and she thought Gaz would have definitely approved, he had liked jokes and laughter, that much she did know about him.

"I'm not sure if Mr Greenwood knows what us vicars get up to these days, but he asked me specifically to refrain from using this 'once-in-a-lifetime' moment as an opportunity to convert anybody." Reverend Cooper raised his hands, palms up. "Rest assured, I will get my fix later today, when I will partake in a Church of England expedition to the wilderness of Worthing."

There were more laughs, somebody cheered.

When the laughing died down, Reverend Cooper started speaking again, his face and voice now serious. "Having promised to ignore my concern for your souls, doesn't mean you get off scot-free. I know what Gary Slater believed in, he and I had that in common, and I think some aspects of our faith are very relevant, here, today. "

Reverend Cooper paused, to throw a sad glance at Gaz's coffin.

"So if you hear me reference our faith, please assume I'm not speaking to you, but that my words are for Gary, or Gaz, as many of you knew him."

There were nods of agreement.

"I knew Gary," Reverend Cooper continued. "He was a regular at the Real Junk Food Café, held weekly at St Luke's in Prestonville. He also came to the Sunday Service there. We often talked of many matters. I was, and am, proud to call him a friend."

There were murmurs of appreciation.

"Alas, he didn't always bring out the best in me..."

Puzzled looks. A few frowns.

"...for there were times when I was guilty of envy..."

"We're all sinners down in Brighton, Reverend," Mr Greenwood said.

"Hear, hear," Tamara added.

"Amen." Reverend Cooper beamed at them. "You're getting the hang of this Tom, and I haven't even started properly yet."

There was resounding laughter.

"Touché." Mr Greenwood said with a wry grin.

Gaz would have loved this!

"Envy is a sin, yes," Reverend Cooper said. "And so I stand before you, a humble sinner. I'm no better than any of you. Nor worse. I am a human being, subject to the struggle of life like everybody else. I too, have wrestled with personal demons."

"Amen!" Somebody in the chapel shouted, and it was taken up by others.

"I must confess that there were times that I envied Gary. Gaz. My friend. Your friend...Our friend."

Confused frowns. People looked at each other, their faces asking why a reverend would envy a homeless man.

"Well," Tamara declared. "He did often hang out in those big windowed alcoves on the West Street side of the Brighton Centre."

"Bloody penthouses, those are," Big John called out.

Reverend Cooper smiled. "It wasn't because of his 'penthouse', I assure you. I envied him because of his faith. I have never known Gary's faith, his trust in a better future, or his contagious optimism to falter."

"True, that," Hailey called out.

Others in the chapel nodded, or murmured their agreement.

"It often gave me cause for thought," Reverend Cooper continued. "Gary's faith was as strong as oak, as resolute as steel. The Lord knows Gary has had his run of misfortune, but whatever life threw at him, his faith stayed rock solid. It could not, it would not be dislodged. I have asked myself, if I had to endure just a portion of the daily dose of injustice Gary was subjected to, would I have had the strength to believe so strongly? To trust in my God? To keep trusting?"

He paused. The chapel was silent.

"I also came upon an answer to that question, and the answer shows how foolish I was to envy. I concluded that it didn't matter if I was as strong as Gary was, *as long as I tried to be...*"

Some in the audience stomped on the floor with their feet.

"With the envy gone, that just left the admiration. I admired Gary, for his faith, his cheer, his constant concern for others...including those who had a roof over their heads, a place to call home. Gary didn't differentiate between the housed and the homeless. To his mind, we were all God's children, deserving of help if we needed it."

"Hear! Hear!" Mr Greenwood called out enthusiastically, and some people applauded.

"Oh! But he is good," Hailey said in wonder.

"When I heard the news, last week, I was...I was..." The reverend stumbled over his words, swallowed, and then took a deep breath. "I was devastated. Simply devastated."

Nods all around.

"At first, I mourned for his loss, as a friend, as a good man. Then I learned the true extent of the tragedy surrounding Gary's death. By rights, by moral obligation, by common human decency, Gary should have been offered a place of respite when he was discharged from the hospital."

"Yes!" Big John cried out.

Reverend Cooper continued. "In a hotel or a bed & breakfast. Failing all that, at least in an emergency winter shelter. I don't think anyone who stepped out of doors over the last few weeks could have failed to notice the bitter wind and icy temperatures. I understand that there were funds, there were places, and that solemn promises were made…yet when Gary was discharged, all that was offered to him was a lonely death on the cold streets."

"Shame!" Tamara called out. "Shame!"

Her words were followed by growls and boos. Someone in the back seats started sobbing loudly.

"Gary's death was preventable, it need not have happened," Reverend Cooper continued. "The loss of a loved one is hard enough to cope with. It becomes unbearable when it strikes sudden, it strikes unexpected, and it takes from us those whom we admire and respect. People who have, in our estimation, *earned* life."

Hailey murmured her approval, others did too.

"For a while, I was furious. I forgot that it isn't my call, or your call, to decide who deserves life or not. I was aghast. I was appalled. I was angry, so angry that I didn't know what to do, and I prayed to God to guide me, to send me a sign."

The reverend paused again. His face, which had been intense, relaxed, and his eyes began to twinkle. "Not less than an hour later, my doorbell rang…"

"Oh, no you don't…" Mr Greenwood spluttered.

"…and lo and behold! By coincidence, or by Divine design, I found Tom Greenwood on my doorstep."

He winked at Mr Greenwood, and there was laughter all around.

"Don't you go involving me now…" Mr Greenwood protested.

"Ah, but you involved me, Tom. You told me of a small miracle, the chance to pay our proper respects to Gary Slater, as human beings. Then you asked me to speak, and I was honoured and humbled to be asked."

"Good on you, Rev," someone in the back of the chapel called out.

"And in doing so, Tom, you may have saved me from my doubts." The reverend smiled.

"The Lord works in mysterious ways, Rev," Tamara called out.

Amy held her breath, wondering if Hailey was going to scream, but she just laughed, along with many others.

"And finds allies in unexpected quarters." Reverend Cooper agreed.

Mr Greenwood muttered, but kept his protest inaudible.

"The request, to speak today, forced me to think anew, rather than just give in to my emotions. I knew what I had been thinking, as Gary's friend. Searching for an answer to the question 'WHY'. Why was Gary taken from us? What possible purpose could his death serve? Why?"

Why? I want to know that too. Why? I didn't save him just so that he could die a few days later.

"In searching for that answer," the reverend continued. "I couldn't avoid the conclusion that this world is far from perfect, and that injustice is a daily occurrence for many."

There were shouts of agreement, which the reverend hushed by raising a hand.

"I called somebody I know in the Council, to put to her, that Gary had received no assistance whatsoever in the end, despite there being a legal, and moral obligation to provide help. I was told that it was all far more complicated than..."

There were boos and growls. Hailey hissed. The reverend waited patiently for the din to die down again.

"It was more complicated than simply lending a helping hand, with protocols, reviews, regulatory updates, and whatnot to consider. We argued the matter for some time, but didn't achieve a compromise. I believe, that sometimes simplicity is a strength, rather than a weakness. Do we not all know good when we encounter it? Do we not all know evil?"

Amy nodded, recalling Frances's outburst to her parents around the Wheatley dinner table, that eleven-year-olds were old enough to know right from wrong, and wrong from right.

"To use the words of a colleague of mine, Reverend Dr. Martin Luther King Jr..."

"I have a dream," somebody said. Others repeated the call. "I have a dream!" "I have a dream!"

"Who's he?" Amy wondered out loud.

"What do they teach you in school these days?" Hailey asked. "He was a great man in America, a man of the people. He dreamed of a better world."

"And was shot for daring to do so," Mr Greenwood added curtly.

"Dr King," the reverend continued. "Was clear on matters of laws and injustice. He said that any law that uplifts the human personality is *just*. Any law that degrades human personality is *unjust*. I say, if a man dies because the laws to save him are too complex to actually do that, then something is wrong with that law."

There were cheers at that, more stomping of feet.

"This is not new, not new at all," Reverend Cooper said. "Even if it may not seem so all the time, God cares about these matters. God didn't become human in the form of Jesus Christ only to teach about love and peace, but also to feel the full impact of the human experience. In his time on earth, Jesus experienced the same bureaucratic intransigence, unnecessary hardship, intolerance and injustice that Gary had to cope with."

The reverend turned to the coffin, and laid his hand upon the lid again. "Gary, Psalm 23 says 'Though I walk through the valley of the shadow of death, you are with me.' For me, this means that God walks alongside us in every aspect of our humanity, especially when that walk is particularly tough. As such, he has walked along with you, Gary, suffered the cold with you, and paid the ultimate price that injustice could exact."

He turned back to face the chapel. "I believe that the Lord will have had a reason to call Gary away from us, but I have not yet been able to figure out what that reason was."

"They have warm beds in private rooms in Heaven," somebody suggested.

Reverend Cooper smiled. He seemed entirely unworried by all the disruptions. "It is my belief that Gary is there now, in a warm bed, in a safe room of his very own."

Amy liked that idea.

"But what if he gets to the pearly gates, and is turned away because he has no local connections?" Big John called out.

The chapel exploded into laughter, all but the reverend, who did at least smile, Amy's father, who looked mildly shocked, and the funeral director who looked like she was about to faint.

"Fortunately," Reverend Cooper continued, after the laughter died down. "The Kingdom of God is all around us. I can assure you a local connection is the last thing that will be asked for at Heaven's gate. Rather, you will be asked what kind of a person you were or tried to be. And in that, you need not be as strong as a Gary, as determined as a Tom Greenwood, as caring as a Tamara, as long as you have *strived* to be those things, *strived* to do the right thing. Dr King said that each and every one of us has a personal choice to make in this life, whether to walk in the light, or walk in the darkness. This applies to all human beings, regardless of whether they are Christian or not."

"Dr. King also said that the ultimate tragedy is not the oppression and cruelty by the bad people, but silence from the good people, when bad things happen. I cannot, at this moment, tell you *why* Gary was taken from us, because the pain of grief weighs heavily on my mind still. What *I* can do, what *you* can do, is to make that personal choice Dr King talked about, whether to walk in light or darkness. What *we* can do, is recognise that in the absence of a meaning which we can understand, we can honour Gary by giving meaning to his passing ourselves. We can speak up, we can strive for a better world, we can fight. And not only can we do these things, we have a moral duty to do so, no matter what your faith is...or isn't, because that it is what makes us human, all of us, together."

The reverend paused, to take a deep breath before he continued. "Dr. King described the Parable of the Good Samaritan as follows. The first question which the priest and the Levite asked was: 'If I stop to help this man, what will happen to *me?*' On the other hand, the question asked by the Samaritan was 'If I do not stop to help this man, what will happen to *him*?' I know what Gary would have asked, because he always gave his concern for others a higher priority than anything related to himself."

"Gary liked to cite the following words from Matthew, because he could relate to them: 'For I was hungry and you gave me food, I was thirsty and you gave me drink, I was a stranger and you welcomed me, I was naked and you clothed me, I was sick and you visited me, I was in prison and you came to me'."

Those words met with a buzz of approval.

"Gary believed that all should open their hands wide to their brothers and sisters, to the needy and the poor. He believed that those who closed their eyes to their brothers and sisters in need, were not open to God's love. He believed that you should love your neighbour as yourself. He liked to cite 'Let us not love in word or talk, but in deed and in truth'. I ask you to consider these words. Not because they are in the Bible, nor because I have repeated them here, but because Gary believed in them, and tried to live his life by them."

Reverend Cooper paused, then said: "I would like to ask all of you to join me, around the coffin, to say your last farewell to Gary."

Everybody rose, and made their way to Gaz's coffin. When they had all gathered around it, Reverend Cooper spoke again.

"Let us commend Gary Slater to the mercy of God, our maker and redeemer. Go forth upon your journey from this world, O Christian soul; in the name of God the Father Almighty who created you; in the name of Jesus Christ who suffered death for you; in the name of the Holy Spirit, who strengthens you; in communion with the blessed saints, aided by angels and archangels and all the heavenly host. May you dwell this day in peace. Amen."

Amy stared at the coffin. It really struck home now. The finality of it. She felt her eyes water. Beside her, Hailey began to shake lightly, tears running down her face. Amy took Hailey's hand, Frances took the other. Hailey kept her eyes on Gaz's coffin, but gently squeezed Amy's hand as a sign of acknowledgement

The reverend continued: "Support us, O Lord, all the day long of this troublous life, until the shadows lengthen and the evening comes, the busy world is hushed, the fever of life is over and our work is done. Then Lord, in your mercy grant us a safe lodging, a holy rest, and peace at last; through Christ our Lord."

Some in the group around the coffin responded with: "Amen."

Mr Greenwood rested a hand on the coffin, and others followed suit, until it seemed that everyone had a hand resting on the coffin, including Amy, Frances and Hailey.

The wood felt smooth beneath Amy's hand. She felt a strong sense of togetherness. There were no more interruptions or jokes, just a group of silent people, united by their sense of loss and the pain of grief, yet strengthened by each other.

Farewell, Gaz.

Reverend Cooper intoned solemnly: "We have entrusted our brother Gary to God's mercy, and we now commit his body to be cremated: earth to earth, ashes to ashes, dust to dust: in sure an certain hope of the resurrection to eternal life through our Lord Jesus Christ, who will transform our frail bodies that they may be conformed to His glorious body, who died, was buried, and rose again for us. To Him be glory for ever."

Just about everybody responded with "Amen" this time.

Earth to earth.

They all stepped back far enough for the reverend and Mr Greenwood to slowly draw the curtains around the coffin.

Ashes to ashes.

It was over.

Dust to dust.

People started to drift toward the entrance to collect their belongings piled up at the back, some gathering around Clare, to get a last hot drink to take outside.

Hailey had sat down again, and the girls joined her, holding her hands again as they shared her grief.

Amy could hear many people thanking Mr Greenwood profusely, remarking how fine it had been to be able to say goodbye. Others thanked Reverend Cooper. Some apologised for the noisy interruptions. The reverend kept on replying that it had been a memorable experience, and an honour to be part of it.

At long last, Hailey rose, and the girls got up too. There were less people in the chapel now, most had gone back out onto the cold streets. Dad, Mr Greenwood, and Reverend Cooper were near the door, deeply engaged in conversation.

Hailey walked towards them, followed by the girls.

"I cannot believe the Crowdfunder," Mr Greenwood said. "People keep on giving. We passed the target within days, but the money keeps on flowing in. I've emailed donors, to tell them we had the funeral covered, but they insist we keep it. Some have suggested a memorial."

"A memorial?" Reverend Cooper asked. "Now that's interesting."

"It'd be interesting," Mr Greenwood declared, "if a memorial had some practical use as well. It's war out there, Rev. I kid you not

"Mr...Reverend Cooper," Hailey said. "I want to thank you for your words...you spoke well. Gaz would have really appreciated it."

Reverend Cooper smiled. "Thank you. I should expect that you'll have more reasons than most to miss Gary.

Hailey nodded I answer.

"Well, you're always welcome at St Luke's.

Hailey smiled wryly. "Rev, I'd come for a cuppa, a dry place to sit. That's all

"Like I said, you're welcome at St Luke's," the reverend smiled. "For a cuppa only, if need be, but also maybe just to talk about Gary. I know I should like to do so."

"Thank you," Hailey said. "I may take you up on that."

Mr Greenwood addressed Amy: "We're hosting a Christmas lunch, on Christmas Eve. Reverend Cooper here has made St Luke's available, so that'll be a nice change from the Clock Tower. I could use some help, if you'd be willing..."

"Say yes!" Frances exclaimed.

Amy was flustered by the question. "Of course I'd like to...but...the..." She looked from Mr Greenwood to her father. To her utter delight, he nodded.

"Your mother and I have agreed that by then you will have been grounded long enough. It seems there won't be much mischief you could get up to, and it'll be a controlled situation."

"Splendid!" Reverend Cooper said. "It'll be good to see you all again."

26. Christmas Eve on Old Shoreham Road

St Luke's in Prestonville was a red bricked building, with stone and stucco dressings, and a steepled corner tower. It sat astride of a long ridge which offered spectacular views of the rows of rising and descending rooftops of Preston Park, Hollingdean and Hanover.

Dad dropped Amy off in front of the church, and reminded her that he'd be back to pick her up, before he drove off again.

Amy walked into the church. Once inside, she could see evidence in the aisles that the church was used as a busy community centre: A children's play corner, bookshelves, arts and crafts materials, and noticeboards filled with reminders about meetings, rehearsals and planned events. Amy spotted a notice about the Real Junk Food Café, which Reverend Cooper had mentioned at the funeral.

The nave was empty, but Big John and other members of Mr Greenwood's team were busy setting up tables and chairs there. It was only the chancel at the far end of the church that served as a reminder that the building was also a place of worship.

Big John greeted Amy cheerfully, and pointed towards an open door, on the far side of the chancel, right by the tea and coffee counter.

There was a small kitchen through there, in which Amy found Mr Greenwood, Tamara, and Frances hard at work, unpacking food from boxes, crates and containers.

"Twenty turkeys!" Mr Greenwood proclaimed proudly when he spotted Amy.

"Like we've only heard that a hundred times today, Dad," Frances said, before greeting Amy with a quick hug.

"Courtesy of Anthony and his people at Bridgers Farm," Mr Greenwood said, almost purring with pleasure.

"Meaning our lads and lasses can have a proper Christmas meal," Tamara said. "It's hard enough on them, this whole bloody festive period."

Amy was put to work, helping Frances unpack and prepare various foodstuffs. Someone had switched on a music system connected to speakers throughout St Luke's, and the girls were soon singing along to a collection of Christmas pop hits.

Amy thought about Tamara's words as she worked and sang. So far, her main concern about the time of year had been the plummeting temperatures. Now, she also realised that the whole notion of Christmas couldn't be easy either. Everywhere you looked, there were reminders in the form of Christmas decorations, festive lights, and seasonal shop displays. A time for cheer, goodwill, and...family.

What must it be like, to be outside in the cold all day, watching the happy anticipation of Christmas shoppers, surrounded by reminders that it was the season to be jolly?

Those thoughts gave Amy extra motivation to do her very best. This afternoon at St Luke's was probably the closest that many of the homeless guests would experience to having any sort of Christmas at all. She wanted to make it as special as possible.

She and Frances were sent out to lay out the tables. They had just finished arranging the red and green paper table cloths when Hailey arrived, a bit earlier to lend a helping hand. She was dressed in the outfit she had worn to visit Gaz in hospital and the funeral, and had made a real effort to do her make-up and her hair.

"Almost human," she laughed, when she noticed Amy admiring her. "The Office had a box full of make-up...it's been a while."

"Really beautiful," Amy said, causing Hailey to beam.

Hailey helped the girls to arrange plates, glasses, cutlery, and trivets. The finishing touch were the Christmas crackers, and none too soon, because more and more guests started filling the church, depositing their belongings in a corner at the back, and then making a beeline towards the tea and coffee counter. Reverend Cooper had appeared, and was by the main door, welcoming the guests with a jolly smile.

"Ah, young ladies!" Miss Puck came striding towards them, resplendent in another green outfit, and holding two long packages under her arm. "Precisely the people I was looking for."

"Miss Puck!" Amy was pleased to see her. "Merry Christmas!"

"A good Yuletide indeed," Miss Puck looked around her, beaming at all the activity. "Tom invited me to partake in the meal."

"He didn't tell me!" Frances said.

"Ah!" Miss Puck exclaimed. "That might be because he charged me with a top-secret mission."

Mr Greenwood joined them. "What's this about a secret mission?"

Miss Puck winked at him. "Special delivery."

"Oh, yes, of course." Mr Greenwood looked pleased. "I've got you both a present, well, actually, I asked Miss Puck to select them."

"Owls?" Frances's eyes grew wide.

Miss Puck laughed. "Not this time! You can hardly be starving at a special Greenwood Christmas lunch."

"Starved for chocolate," Frances protested.

Miss Puck chuckled, and then reached into her coat to retrieve two packages, long rectangular boxes wrapped in simple brown paper, on which someone had carefully penned:

Amy and *Frances*.

"For us?" Frances asked eagerly

Miss Puck nodded, and handed the packages over. Mr Greenwood watched with twinkling eyes as the girls removed the wrapping paper to reveal two long simple cardboard boxes, the lids tied on with lengths of twine.

"They're Wyrde Woods wand boxes!" Amy cried out.

"Go on! Open them!" Mr Greenwood chuckled.

They gingerly lifted the lids off the boxes, and then stared in amazement at the wands, for they were the very same which they had selected as their all-time favourites back at The Owlery.

"How did you know?" Amy asked in wonder.

Miss Puck looked comically offended for a moment, then said: "Why, magic of course."

"Also called CCTV." Mr Greenwood chuckled again.

"By the Silver Swan!" Miss Puck cried out. "Tom, I'm disappointed in you. Yes, I do happen to have CCTV, but these wands were selected by my magical powers."

"They are so beautiful," Frances had taken her wand out of the box, and waved it in the air. "Thank you, Dad!"

"Thank you Mr Greenwood," Amy said, enthralled by the weight of the wand in her hand when she removed it from the box. "It's almost like they are real."

"Oh what a pair of puckstools you are." Miss Puck shook her head. "Of course they are real, why don't you try them out?"

Frances grinned, and looked at her father. "Can we?"

"Just don't go turning anybody into bloody owls," Mr Greenwood said. "Chocolate or not."

Frances looked around, spotted Big John, flicked her wrist, waved the wand and called out: "SMILUS!"

As if by magic, Big John responded with a wide grin.

"See, it works!" Miss Puck said, beaming with satisfaction.

Amy walked towards Hailey, waved her wand and said: "SMILUS!"

Hailey smiled too, and it would have been impossible to stop the girls after that. They ran around the tables, by the tea and coffee counter, and then past the chancel, flicking their wrists and calling out their spell: "SMILUS!"

Amy was laughing, as she spelled her way towards the door, all worries and concerns forgotten for a moment, as she and Frances conjured up smile after smile.

Out of the corner of her eye, Amy saw two new people come in, she turned, pointed her wand and yelled: "SMILUS!"

The spell only half worked this time. Amy's father responded with a smile, but Mum wasn't smiling at all, instead, she was looking around apprehensively, her mouth drawn tight.

"Mum! Dad! What are you doing here?"

For a brief instant, Amy felt a pang of guilt, until she reminded herself that her parents had given permission for her to be at St Luke's this afternoon. That was followed by Amy's sudden concern that Mum would shout at somebody, as she had shouted at Hailey outside of the London Road Co-Op.

Oh my God, Hailey is here.

"Tom...Mr Greenwood invited us," Dad explained. "And we thought we'd come. The neighbour didn't mind looking after Jacob for a few hours."

"Mr Wheatley, Merry Christmas." It was Hailey who came forward, her hand outstretched. "We met at Gaz's funeral."

Amy's heart skipped a beat.

"So we did." Dad shook her hand "Let me introduce you to my..."

"We've met before," Hailey said.

"We did?" Mum shook her head as if to clear it. "I don't recall..."

"Earlier this month," Hailey explained. "Outside the Co-Op, on London Road.

Mum's mouth fell open. "But...you...I..."

Under any other circumstances, Amy would have smiled at Mum's reaction, but she felt a knot of anxiety in her tummy, hoping that this meeting wouldn't turn foul.

"I dressed up for this occasion," Hailey explained.

Mum turned bright red. "I think I owe you an apology."

Frances and Mr Greenwood joined them. Frances looked at Amy, behind Mr Greenwood's broad back, and made her 'O' face. Amy stifled a nervous giggle.

Hailey shook her head. "Can't say I enjoyed it, but you were right to be concerned, Mrs Wheatley. I'd have been protective of Amy, she's a very special girl."

To Amy's surprise and delight, Mum nodded, and even smiled. "Yes, that she is."

"So many redheads, all in one place," Mr Greenwood rumbled. "I couldn't be more..."

"...Closer to making inappropriate comments, in my church of all places." Reverend Cooper joined the group. "Hello Nancy."

Mum's reaction was remarkable. She turned pale, faltered, and reached out a hand to Dad for support. "Oh my God!"

"Not quite," Reverend Cooper smiled. "Although I do like to think that I speak on His behalf on occasion."

Mum looked at Dad. "You knew?"

Dad nodded. "We met at the funeral, the other day."

"Although Josh was a mite more pleased to see me than you appear to be," Reverend Cooper said, still smiling.

"Oh no! Vincent!" Mum shook her head. "It's not that...I just hadn't been expecting...and...Amy..."

Amy had trouble following it all, but she was intrigued.

"Perhaps," Mr Greenwood said. "We should sit down for a moment?" He indicated the corner opposite the main door, half concealed behind large screens displaying numerous photographs, and a sign which read ART FROM THE EDGE.

There was a stack of chairs by the wall. Dad and Mr Greenwood arranged the chairs into a rough circle, and they all sat down: Amy, Mum, Dad, Frances, Mr Greenwood, and Reverend

Cooper. Hailey made to move away, but Mr Greenwood insisted she join them too.

Amy looked around the circle of people, full of wonder. Mum still looked shaken, and Dad was holding her hand.

What is going on? More trouble?

"There is something we've been meaning to tell you, Amy," Dad said solemnly.

Amy looked at Frances, but her friend shrugged her shoulders and looked just as curious as Amy felt.

"Do you want to, Nancy?" Reverend Cooper asked. "Or shall I?"

"Please." Mum nodded. "If you don't mind."

Reverend Cooper smiled. "I still remember the first time we met, Nancy. Vividly so."

"You must think I've become a horrible person," Mum blurted out.

The reverend looked surprised. "Oh dear me! No. Not at all! Look at you, Josh tells me you've done well. Children, a nice home, a successful career. I'm exceedingly proud of you."

"But…," Mum stammered. "Amy…"

"Now, I don't know about your faith these days." Reverend Cooper smiled. "But I know what my faith is, resolutely so. To see your daughter here in St Luke's, on Christmas Eve, ready to serve those less fortunate…from my perspective it's a Christmas Miracle."

Mum looked so unhappy that Amy was tempted to flick her wand at her and attempt another SMILUS, but she thought better of it.

"It wasn't Christmas," Reverend Cooper continued. "But it was much the same. A Church in London, do you remember Nancy? Tables, chairs, volunteers busily cooking a big meal…"

Mum nodded, and clutched Dad's hand tightly. Amy stared at them, trying to understand.

212

Reverend Cooper continued speaking, in a gentle voice. "When you came in, you were soaking wet, it was raining outside. And you stood there, Nancy, dripping so much water that a puddle formed around your feet. A gaping hole in one boot, jeans torn, your army coat smudged with filth, your hair knotted and tangled...You were afraid to let go of your sleeping bag because you didn't trust anyone anymore."

"WAIT! WHAT?" Amy exclaimed.

Mum wouldn't meet her eyes.

"Mum?! You were homeless?"

Mum nodded.

"But...but...why didn't you tell me?"

Mum looked up now, to meet Amy's eyes.

"It was...children can be so indiscreet, they talk freely to friends, teachers, neighbours..."

"You're ashamed?" Hailey asked.

Amy was suddenly struck by how alike Mum and Hailey were. It wasn't just the red hair, but more the way they carried themselves, always with their guards up, always wary, and only now and then accidentally showing the cracks in their armour.

"Yes," Mum said, almost defiantly. "I am ashamed. It's not a period of my life I look back at with pride, or nostalgic feelings, other than Josh of course.

Amy looked at Dad with wide eyes. "You saved her?"

Dad grinned sheepishly. "No, I was in a worse state than your mum, truth be told. She saved me."

"You too?" Amy could barely believe it, as her mind struggled to work through all this new information. They had been so...so dead set against anything to do with homelessness, but they had known, they had known all this time.

"I work at a law firm," Mum said to Hailey, in what seemed partially a challenge and partially an apology. "Homelessness is associated..."

"With junkies and drunks," Hailey said bitterly.

Mum nodded. "When I first saw you, outside the Co-Op, it was...it was like looking in a mirror and seeing myself. I have tried so hard to forget. I don't need to tell you what it's like out there, it's dangerous, it's...it's not safe. Not safe. That's why I didn't want Amy...I don't want Amy to ever..."

It isn't safe. Not safe. It's like hearing Hailey say those words on London Road.

Mum buried her face in her hands, and began to sob. To Amy's surprise, Hailey rose from her chair, walked towards Amy's mother, kneeled by her side, and then wrapped her arms around her. Mum hugged back, and Hailey slowly rocked her to and fro, as if Mum were just a small child.

Somehow, the sight of Mum crying like that was even more shocking to Amy than all she had just heard. She looked at Frances, who had been following everything in uncharacteristic silence. Frances looked back, too flabbergasted to even form that 'O' of hers.

Amy looked around. Mr Greenwood was studying his fingernails. Reverend Cooper's eyes were on the church roof rafters as if he had never seen them before. Dad was looking at Mum and Hailey, a sad smile on his face.

"Dad," Amy said. "You should've told me before...after...I understand that it was difficult...but..."

"It's made things more complicated," Dad admitted. "And unnecessarily tense. We've talked about it, and owe you a big apology."

Amy nodded, but still felt cheated somehow.

"I'm nearly twelve now," she said. "And I can keep secrets."

"Yes, I believe you can," Dad acknowledged, but then added, somewhat stricter: "But you've also shown great potential to get yourself into trouble, don't think that..."

"Peas in a pod, Josh," Mr Greenwood rumbled. "Peas in a pod. Just you wait, they'll turn our greying hair white with worry. We could put them up for adoption? Save ourselves all that misery?"

"Dad!" Frances protested. "Remember the expensive therapist I'm going to need. This'll be at least half-a-dozen extra sessions."

Amy's father looked puzzled at that, and Amy tried not to smile. She looked down, at the wand she was still holding in her hands.

SMILUS!

Amy smiled. Sometimes there really wasn't much else you could do, she reckoned. She had a lot of questions she wanted to ask, accusations she wanted to make, but...right now Mum was upset. Wilf would have rubbed his fluffy head against her leg. Gaz would have offered to make her a cup of tea. Amy looked at Reverend Cooper and recalled what he had said about not thinking of 'me', but of others. She remembered how upset she had been when Mum had told her to ignore Hailey's plight on London Road. Could she now ignore Mum's upset, when she had been haunted by a stranger's pain?

Amy got up, walked towards Mum and Hailey, and joined their hug.

"It's alright, Mum," Amy said. "It's gonna be alright."

Mum's shoulders shook, but then she looked up, with a smile on her face despite the tears.

"Group hug!" Frances shouted, and shot off her chair to join in.

"I'll pass, thank you," Mr Greenwood said. He glanced at his watch, and then behind them, where most guests were seated now, holding mugs of tea or coffee, the buzz of their talk filled with happy anticipation.

"Right," Mum said. "I'll be okay now."

The others let go of her. She wiped at her eyes furiously with her sleeves.

"Nancy," Reverend Cooper asked. "Would you like to…"

"What I'd like to do," Mum said, with growing determination in her voice. "Is to lend a hand. Mr Greenwood, can you use another volunteer?"

"Me too," Dad said quickly.

Amy looked at them both in wonder. Whatever the reverend said, this was the true Christmas miracle for Amy.

Mr Greenwood smiled his broadest smile. "I thought you'd never ask, come on, I'll quickly show you around. Girls…"

"Yes, Dad?"

"Yes, Mr Greenwood."

"Ready for some more child labour?"

"Aye aye, Cap'n," Amy said.

"Under protest," Frances added.

"Duly noted," Mr Greenwood agreed. "Come, there's work to be done."

27. Starling's Dance at Palace Pier

Amy wandered out onto the decking of Palace Pier.

Dad and Mr Greenwood had asked Amy and Frances to meet them at the pier, but there was no sign of them yet. Amy didn't have a clue as to why the fathers had arranged the meeting. Despite a barrage of questions and wild guesses, both men had responded only with silence and infuriatingly mysterious smiles.

Frances was inside one of the arcades. She had circled the 2p pusher machines like a lioness prowling about a herd of antelopes, until she had spotted a likely victim, and pounced.

"They build these things to make you lose," Amy had told her friend, as Frances started throwing in 2p coins.

"Maybe," Frances had said, and then added, in a deep movie preview voiceover: "But they have not counted on Miss Frances Greenwood, who has yet to play a losing round on a 2p machine."

After that Frances had focused so intently on the game that it seemed to Amy that her friend had forgot about the entire world, apart from herself and the 2p machine. Amy had given it a try, but lost interest after losing a handful of 2p coins, after which she had wandered out of the arcade, onto the decking.

The sun was beginning to sink into the clouds on the western horizon, outlining the silhouettes of grand seafront hotels, the towering i360, Shoreham Power Station, and the ghostly remnants of West Pier against a backdrop of fiery gold, red and orange. There was a scattering of low level clouds stretching all the way to Rottingdean, and these too began to light up, until the entire horizon became a broad band of bright, fusing colours.

A cloud of starlings were gathering between Palace Pier and West Pier, attracting smaller flights of starlings which joined the greater whole. The dark cloud of small specks grew, and started to pulsate, veering left, then wheeling right, before one such protrusion kept on flying, and was followed by the rest of the murmuration. The birds swooped and whirled in perfect unison, their mass sometimes losing darkness as the murmuration threatened to break apart, and sometimes flying so densely that they truly appeared to be a single being.

The murmuration danced above the sea for some time, before heading towards Palace Pier at some speed, breaking apart when they reached the pier. A considerable number of starlings streaked by below Amy, to disappear between the piles below the pier's decking, but the greater part of the murmuration passed by overhead. Amy looked up, and her entire vision was filled with sky and swooping starlings. She could see them individually now, though not in focus, because of the sheer speed with which they passed. Soon after, the murmuration came swooping back again, above and below Palace Pier.

Watching them was hypnotising, and Amy had no idea how long she stood there, leaning on the railing, before the murmuration took off for West Pier to become a vague smudge on the horizon, which was slowly taking on mostly purple and pink hues now.

"LOOK WHAT I WON!" Frances walked towards Amy, clutching a plastic bag. She opened the bag to let Amy peer in, and started listing her winnings. "Four clown heads. Three Pokémon key rings. Five 'B-Right-On!' stickers. Two bear figurines. And two mugs!"

"Straight to Aladdin's cave," Amy said, shaking her head. "Except for the stickers, those are slick."

Frances formed her 'O' expression. "Amy! These are treasures, don't you get it? TREASURES! Precioussss. All mine."

Amy frowned dubiously. "The mugs say 'I Love Brighton Pier'."

Her friend's shoulders sagged. "Yeah, well, there is that."

They started walking towards the pier's entrance.

"I wouldn't be seen dead drinking out of anything that says Brighton Pier," Amy said.

Frances brightened up. "We could sell them to tourists this summer. Make a killing. I'll ask Dad for a stall at the Open Market."

"A stall for two mugs?"

"Of course not. Don't be silly. I'll come back to the Palace Pier every day to play the 2p machines. We'll have a massive stock to sell. What shall we call our shop?"

"Young Mugs," Amy said, and they laughed. "Tell me again, about Hailey."

"Amy, I've told you twice already."

"Pretty please!"

"Someone from the Brighton and Hove Housing Coalition has advocated for her. Which means..."

"...spoken on her behalf. You eleven-point-two-fivers might not get that, but eleven-point-fivers definitely understand."

"You're deffo daft, you are. Anyway, they've offered Hailey a place to stay."

"A place to stay," Amy said dreamily.

"Yeah, well, don't expect too much from it, it's emergency accommodation."

"It must be better than a shop doorway!" Amy protested.

Frances sighed, as melodramatically as she could. "For an eleven-pointless-fiver, you have a lot to learn."

They reached the pier gates, and walked onto the pavement beyond.

"Where are they?" Frances complained. "I'm a busy woman."

"Busy doing what?" Amy asked, because Christmas Break had left them gloriously free.

"Playing 2p machines, investing in our business."

An odd bus pulled up by the side of Madeira Drive. A double-decker bus in orange livery, aged and somewhat battered. Its smaller front destination blind read '3'. The main rollsign with destination names was moving.

...Rottingdean...Bevendean...Woodingdean...Moulsecoomb...

"I don't think he knows where he wants to go," Amy pointed.

...Coldean...Stanmer Heights...Hollingbury...Patcham...

Frances looked.

...Whitehawk...Hove...Portslade...

"If he's from out of town," Frances said. "I've got some mugs to sell to him."

...Kemptown...Brighton...

The next and last name, the letters less neat because they were hand-painted, made them blink, and then gasp.

...GAZ...

The driver of the bus honked his horn, a man standing next to the driver's seat, beckoned them impatiently.

The man waving was Dad, the driver Mr Greenwood.

"Oh my God!" Frances exclaimed. "He's gone and done it."

"Done what?"

"Bought a bus."

"Bought a bus!? I don't understand why, to carry donations?"

"Don't you see!" Frances was grinning from ear-to-ear. "Bunk-beds, a toilet, a kitchen, a living room!"

"You mean..?"

"It's gonna be a homeless shelter. I'll bet you two Brighton Pier mugs for your brother."

"Okay," Amy said absentmindedly. She looked at the bus in wonder. "Can they really do that?

Mr Greenwood honked again.

"Let's go and find out!" Frances tugged at Amy's arm. The two girls ran to the big orange bus called Gaz, and towards their next adventure.

THE END

Acknowledgements

Books are never written alone. We couldn't have possibly completed this story in the time that we did without all the help we received, and would like to express our sincere gratitude to the following people

Thank you to Annie Fletcher and Janet Going, from Invisible Voices of Brighton & Hove, for suggesting in the first place that we try our hand at translating the housing crisis in our city into a fictional story for readers young and old.

Thank you to Frances Deans and Aisling Bodley, for your unique perspective as experts in being kids. Your feedback has been invaluable

Thank you Famke Kalkman, for following this story from its conception to the end, and providing feedback and suggestions up to the extent that you practically became the third author of this story

Thank you Debbie Shipton, for your detailed copy editing, spotting all those glaring little mistakes which we somehow missed.

Thank you Nicole den Heeten, Janet Going, Sue Lewis, Colette Chitty, Elina Langley, and Julia Nye, for letting us test our story on you, for your feedback, and much needed encouragement.

A special thank you to Johanna, for appearing as yourself. Tragically, Wilf is no longer with us, and it can't have been easy to help us recreate him on the pages of this book. We are so pleased he is part of it though, and grateful to you for helping us portray him and yourself correctly.

Another special thank you is also due to Reverend Martin Poole, on whom the character of Reverend Vincent Cooper is based. Reverend Poole has been most helpful in offering advice and guidance with regard to the funeral in the story, and many of the words spoken by Reverend Cooper on that occasion have been provided by Reverend Poole.

Last-but-not-least, we are especially indebted to Jim and Frances Deans. These two remarkable people and their efforts to ease the situation of Brighton's unfortunate homeless formed the inspiration for this book, as have the many volunteers who support Jim and Frances through Sussex Homeless Support.

All proceeds from this book have been pledged to Cascade Creative Recovery, First Base & Sussex Homeless Support.

A sequel, entitled *Back on Brighton Streets*, is highly likely. Keep an eye out on the Invisible Voices Facebook page for any news on this.

A last note on a deliberate inaccuracy: 'Public Safety Enforcement Officers' are currently fictional, however, their introduction is being discussed by the powers that be.

By the by, we LOVE reviews. The number of reviews received on places like Amazon and GoodReads are crucial these days, as they are often the measurement used to determine the success of a book. Reviews need not be overly complicated, just a mention that the book was enjoyed or is recommended is absolutely fine and would be most gratefully received

Nils Nisse Visser & Cair Emma Going
Brighton, April 2018.

If you would like to meet the authors in person, we can often be found at the Clock Tower Street Kitchen on Sundays, in practical support of Sussex Homeless Support.

If you enjoyed *ON BRIGHTON STREETS* you may enjoy another Brighton story by Nisse Visser. *WILL'S WAR IN BRIGHTON* follows the experiences of Will Maskall and his friends during the 1940 Brighton Blitz. Based on first-hand accounts and local anecdotes and recollections.

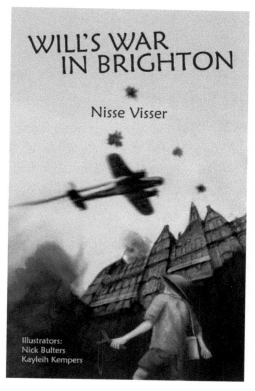

For further stories by Nils Nisse Visser, please visit:
http://www.nilsnissevisser.co.uk/

INVISIBLE VOICES OF BRIGHTON & HOVE

Invisible Voices of Brighton & Hove was founded in 2016. The aim of this group is to raise awareness regarding local homeless issues, and also to raise funds in support of effective local charities. One way of raising awareness is to give a voice to those who so often remain unheard in our community, by creating an opportunity for vulnerable people to speak out in various ways during the Brighton Fringe Festivals.

For Fringe 2016, we organised a photography exhibition, as well as publishing two books: *Invisible Voices of Brighton & Hove* and *Born and Bred*. The first book being a collection of interviews, journal records, personal stories and poetry, the second poems by street poet extraordinaire Craig Neesam.

For Fringe 2017, we organised another photography exhibition, as well as publishing two further books: *Invisible Voices 2017*, and Craig Neesam's second collection of poems, including contributions by others, called *The Oaks*. We also facilitated a stage show called *Another Brighton*.

For Fringe 2018 there is another photography exhibition, and we hope to publish no less than three books. One is the book you're holding in your hands right now, *On Brighton Streets*, which is our first fictional reflection of the local housing crisis. The other two are further collections of poetry by two poets who contributed work in 2017: *The Queen of Brighton* by Ró Bodley, and *Seasoned Eyes Are Beaming* by Jovannah Bär.

Invisible Voices can be found on Facebook, or their website: www.invisiblevoices.co.uk

Lightning Source UK Ltd.
Milton Keynes UK
UKHW02f2221230418
321519UK00001B/5/P